NOBLE ROT

NOBLE ROT

by

John Scherber

The Seventeenth Book in the Murder in Mexico Series

San Miguel Allende Books
San Miguel de Allende, Guanajuato, Mexico

ACKNOWLEDGMENTS

Any book starts as an idea, and by its completion becomes a joint effort.

Thanks to all the following:
Lander Rodriguez for the cover design.
Julio Mendez for website design.

Thanks to Nancy Howze for assistance with locations.
Thanks to Prof. Henry Beckmeyer, MD for assistance on medical issues.
For the cover painting, *Revelación* Oil/canvas 51x69 inches, 2010, thank you to Santigo Corral y Gutiérrez.
For editing and many valuable suggestions: my wife, Kristine Scherber.

This is a work of fiction. Any resemblance to actual persons, living or dead, is entirely coincidental.

ISBN: 978-0-9906551-5-2

San Miguel Allende Books
www.sanmiguelallendebooks.com

Also by John Scherber

FICTION

(The Townshend Vampire Trilogy)
And Dark My Desire
And Darker My Wrath

The Devil's Workshop
Eden Lost
The Amarna Heresy
Beyond Terrorism: Survival

NONFICTION

San Miguel de Allende: A Place in the Heart
*A Writer's Notebook: Everything I Wish Someone Had Told Me
When I Was Starting Out*
*Into the Heart of Mexico: Expatriates Find Themselves off the
Beaten Path*
Living in San Miguel: The Heart of the Matter

It is the chiefest point of happiness that a man is willing to be what he is.

--Desiderius Erasmus

In some ways grape varieties resemble passionate lovers. Not every combination produces a winning blend, and some can even leave a sour taste in your mouth.

--Derek Hamilton,
A Philosophy for Our Time

For Kristine

PROLOGUE

Sebastian Cavaletti stood at the top of the two-story staircase with his arms crossed over his chest. His face was burning and his hands gripped his shoulders as if to literally pull himself together. He could not recall the last time he'd been so angry. How could this have happened? Coming into the room, he had turned the music up a notch to help calm his mind. It was one of his favorite Vivaldi pieces, the guitar concerto in D, but it hadn't helped.

Forcing himself to focus on other things, his eyes scanned the upscale room searching for order, for peace. It was worthy of a person of his stature. The furniture was elegant with classic lines. The art was from several periods, none recent. The staircase at his feet was worthy of a coronation. Uninterrupted, and flanked by no handrails, the limestone treads and risers were formal and unadorned. He could appreciate its classic look, but at the same time it seemed more ceremonial than practical. What about older people? What if they had a momentary dizzy spell? There was nothing to grip to break their fall. The owners of this house he had rented must be young and very rich.

He froze for moment as rage flashed back into his mind. He thrust the thought aside. It was not worth a heart attack or a stroke. It had been a stroke that killed his father fourteen years before.

Sebastian Cavaletti was a wealthy man himself and could've also afforded a grand house like this, but his own winery residence in Northern California was a single story, a rambling and gracious adobe hacienda with tall ceilings. He had opted for comfort over display, a contented informality over grandeur.

Still, this house he was renting was quite suitable for the month he'd be in México, checking out properties to add as a southern branch to the Cavaletti Vineyards. An involuntary smile crossed his face as he caught a favorite passage in the background guitar music. He had tried early in his life to learn the guitar, but without success. Perhaps his absorption was why he didn't hear the soft rush of footsteps behind him. Nor did he feel the impact of the weapon that struck him at the back of his head. The force of it drove him down the long flight of limestone stairs head over heels, but he was beyond feeling anything by then. His head sharply struck the limestone treads three times before Sebastian Cavaletti ended his life in a misshapen pile at the bottom of the steps.

CHAPTER ONE

When my house phone rang at eight o'clock that morning I was already finished with breakfast. The call came in on the Paul Zacher Agency line, so I knew what kind of business it was going to be. The indignant voice of an elderly woman greeted me without ceremony on the other end.

"Are you Paul Zacher? If you're not, then put me through to him immediately! I don't have time to waste talking to some lackey. I've been ejected from my home and I want something done about it. Furthermore, my nephew is dead from a fall!"

A substantial beginning, I thought, even if the tone was off, although I couldn't help but notice the order of importance in her listing of those events.

"OK, ma'am, hold on so I can write this down." I gripped the phone with my chin while I located a pad and a pen in a drawer in the kitchen. "First of all, this is the real Paul Zacher you've reached. We don't use any lackeys here. Who am I speaking with, please?"

"This is Rachel Cavaletti (she spelled out both names), from Healdsburg, California. That's in Sonoma County. My nephew, Sebastian, died in a fall on the stairs last night and the police have ejected us from our rental home here in San Miguel. I don't even have a tooth-brush. I'm calling from the Overlook Palace Hotel."

This was a decidedly upscale hostelry near the Parque Juarez, not far from downtown, the area we call *centro*.

"I'm sure if you ask at the concierge desk, they'll give you some toiletries. They have those little kits for situations like this."

"Do you know the police here?"

"Better than I want to sometimes. Was it Licenciado Diego Delgado who put you out of your house?"

"Yes. And I found you because of that article in *Modern Vintner* last month."

Modern Vintner had done a feature piece on our annual wine and food festival here in San Miguel de Allende, México. Along with these monthly regional event articles they always ran a sidebar, as we were told when they called me, titled *Local Color*. It featured photos and a couple of paragraphs on three personalities or groups that in their view somehow personified the spirit of the town or region. It was late in February when they came through and only a couple of weeks since we'd solved the murder of the San Miguel painter, Edward Jericho. It had made a minor impact and they had seen the headline news in the local press. They decided the Paul Zacher Agency made a good human interest story, along with the head of the opera society, and the leader of a charity that built free houses for homeless families. We weren't displeased to have the publicity. This call confirmed its value.

"OK. Give me a few minutes and I'll call Delgado and see whether just for some place to start I can get you back into your house."

"Thank you, young man. I shall be waiting for your call."

This looked easy enough, and I didn't plan to charge her anything for this service. It never hurts to spread a little goodwill, and handing out a few low cost freebees eases the way.

Four hours later, after Rachel Cavaletti and her party had been reinstalled in their rental house and had a chance to clean up and change clothes, Maya Sanchez (my partner in life and in the Agency), and I were sitting in their great room for a meeting with Miss Rachel that she had requested. I had so quickly gotten the Cavalettis back into their house not because I had any profound influence with law enforcement here, but because Licenciado Delgado of the Judicial Police had finished gathering the physical evidence in what looked like a simple fall down a difficult flight of steps. He had found little for him and his crew to take away, aside from the contorted body of Sebastian Cavaletti. Because we encountered him on most of the cases we worked, our relationship was usually easy and cordial, even when, as sometimes happened, we ended up on opposite sides of a case.

The room where Maya and I sat was grand in scale, with a twenty-foot-high beamed ceiling, and about twenty-five feet in width and fifty feet long. The half that was most distant from the fireplace held an antique pool table. We had seen when I wrote down the address that the Cavalettis had acquired this rental in a very upscale part of town.

In her restless pacing, Miss Rachel paused near the fireplace, her cane in her hand, but she wasn't leaning on it. For this performance it operated more like a pointer, a way to underline key bullet points in her delivery, or to sweep away unwanted comments. She was dressed in an olive-colored pair of slacks and an off-white blouse that appeared rather masculine in character. Her gray hair was drawn tightly into a bun and she wore no jewelry. She might have been five-foot-two in height. When she came in we had quickly moved past the opening introductions.

The room was richly decorated with antique ceramic jars and plates, devotional paintings in remarkable condition, a genuine colonial period chest of drawers, and a fanciful stenciled wood ceiling.

"A horrible man, and so insistent, that Mr. Delgado. You know how tiresome people can be when they think the law is on their side. At home, of course, I would've had our attorney escort him off the property immediately." Miss Rachel resumed her emphatic march.

"However," I said, gently, "as a member of the local Judicial Police, he might normally be expected to think…"

"He can damn well think whatever he pleases. I know a few people in this town too, the right kind of people in the wine business." She rammed the point of her cane into the stone tiles of the floor, which were no more receptive or yielding than she was.

Maya sat with her hands pressed together between her knees. She had so far said nothing. She was always put off by this kind of confrontational opening. If she had said anything, it would've been that this is not how business is done in México. Not that it never happened, but when it did, it went nowhere.

"Do you mind if Maya and I pace around the room too?" I said. "I feel like we're trying to catch up with you all the time."

This caused her eyebrows to lift. "Sorry. I'll sit down if it makes you better able to focus on what I'm saying. Senseless events like this make me so angry. I know that no one can replace Sebastian. I had counted on him being around long enough to pass the business on to the boys when they came of age. In my own mind I've been mostly retired since Sebastian took over after his father died."

She sat on the sofa and leaned the cane against the broad arm next to her. I'm sensitive to artifacts, so I couldn't help but study it. With a body made of a dark gnarled wood, highly polished, and a silvery tip at the bottom, the cane was an interesting piece, and obviously far from new. At the top, a branch curved off the main shaft for about five inches to form the grip, before it continued for an inch or two above that intersection. That upper end was encased in a bright metal too, but not silver, I thought. Possibly it could be nickel, with its softer, more antique sheen. If that was the case, her skin appeared not to be sensitive to it, although I knew some people were.

"Do you like my cane?" Miss Rachel said, seeing my look. "It belonged to Jack London, whose ranch is not so far from our vineyard. The shaft is desert iron-wood, I was told, and it came from near Death Valley."

"A wonderful piece," I said. "And so California, too." I'd always thought Death Valley was one of the world's best and most outrageous place names.

"But you're here to talk about Sebastian, I believe?"

"Yes, at your request. Someone in the house must've called the police last night. If Mr. Cavaletti's fall down those steps was merely an accident, phoning for an ambulance would've been a better course of action. At least I was able to get the house reopened quickly."

When a death from an unusual cause is reported to the police here, they seal the house immediately, even in the absence of any evidence of wrongdoing. That gives them a chance to search for clues without interference from residents, who may have some proprietary interest in the outcome.

"Yes, thank you for that. Without it, I fear we all would've still been living on the street."

This was not my idea of the elegant Overlook Palace Hotel, which routinely housed opera singers and cabinet members, but Miss Rachel was under a lot of stress.

"I'm sure you're in a state of shock, Miss Cavaletti," Maya said. "Were you close to your nephew?"

Miss Rachel drew herself up slightly. Her full height in the slippers she was wearing may have been five-foot-two, more than ten inches less than mine. "To tell you the truth, when Sebastian listened to me we got along just fine. Of course, over the years we've had our minor tiffs about a few policy and business issues. But generally it was, well, it has always been an Italian family. We were accustomed to saying what we thought, and nothing remained under the rug. We could always open a bottle of the best reserve when we wanted to patch things up. And that's often what it came to."

"I assume you are part owner of the winery?" Maya said.

"Of course. Sebastian and I each owned forty percent of it, and he's been president for fourteen years now. Because of his death, Elizabeth, his...widow now, would inherit his forty percent, I'm sure. Each of their boys owns ten percent. In this crisis I have taken her under my wing. She's not well, you know."

This kind of statement was too ambiguous to put down in my notebook. "Does she have some chronic condition?" Maya said with a note of sympathy in her voice.

"Chronic, yes, but as for what that is exactly, no one has ever been able to tell us. She's had more tests than the atomic bomb in the fifties. Sebastian often said that her main problem was an addiction to those tests, and if she could be cured of that she'd be just fine."

"Is your husband still alive?" I said, wishing to move on.

Her eyebrows went up at the thought and she pursed her lips, which drew her lined hollow cheeks in further against her teeth. "I have never been married, Mr. Zacher. Not that I wasn't quite the prize in my day. I just never had what I felt was the right offer. I guess you could say I've been married to the business and my family. God knows that has always been a handful." She held up one palm as if to demonstrate its capacity.

"So where did you leave it with Licenciado Delgado?" I said.

"Do you mean where did he leave it with me? When I talked to him by phone shortly before you arrived, he said there might be reason to believe Sebastian's death was a murder."

"Now I'm seeing this better. Did he tell you why he thought that?" Maya said, showing no reaction, but this did not surprise me. In the past Delgado had occasionally made an assumption that a crime existed where none had.

"No, and I did not ask him."

I recognized this as the point where we often entered a case. "So you would like the Paul Zacher Agency to help him solve the crime? We've worked with Delgado before a number of times, and that would not be a problem for either of us."

Miss Rachel rose and drew herself up to her full height. "I want nothing of the kind, Mr. Zacher. The very idea is absurd. I want you to prove that man wrong. It was simply a terrible fall, a tragic accident. You saw the stairs coming in. They very likely go on for two full stories without a break. Fortunately, there is a pair of discreet elevators off the vestibule, one for family and one for staff. Now you can understand how I get up and down here. The tone of that staircase is, well, *ceremonial* is the only word I can think of to describe it. You'd need to have all your wits about you going both ways, and staff at both elbows. It's better not to try it, I say."

I made a note to ask Delgado what the victim's level of blood alcohol had been. The coroner would've measured that routinely.

"But if it wasn't an accident," said Maya, "wouldn't you want to know that?"

"Of course, young lady, but I simply don't believe it." Her sweeping gesture with the cane would've sliced through anyone within two meters of her.

The Zacher Agency had been hired before to help with cover-ups. Thinking of it as hazard pay, we had always charged extra for that. The hazard was a moral one, but no less real.

Miss Rachel settled back onto the sofa. "To help you both understand my position better, let me tell you a story. My immigrant grandfather, Arturo, founded Cavaletti Vineyards. In the beginning it was not a fancy operation, since he did not come from pretentious people at home, but he had the gift of some family money, not a lot, but enough to buy a piece of property at the edge of Healdsburg in Sonoma County. The Cavalettis had made wine in Italy for six generations, and he started with jug wines, peddling them from tavern to restaurant.

Selling them at the local markets. He had a decent product but they were nothing special, and they were cheap. In those early days California meant nothing on a label, and price was everything.

"When Prohibition came he made a display of selling legal table grapes even as he moved his winemaking operation into the woods. He paid off a few key people in local government and he did OK. He survived quite well, and with some reserves to carry him forward." Her tone underlined the final word. "When the Depression came and Prohibition was overturned a few years later, he was ready for it. He had foreseen it. His vines and his means of production were intact and ready to go."

"Humble beginnings," offered Maya with an encouraging smile. Miss Rachel did not appear to either notice or require her support.

"Then in the early sixties, his son, my father, began to realize that in the future, the best money was going to be made in premium wines, estate bottled, and so on. Vintage years and varietal grapes, you get the picture, even down here. He felt that to have the name of California on the label was eventually going to mean something important, and that new generations of wine lovers would come to regard California with the same level of interest they gave to Italy and France. His project became to elevate the image of the Cavaletti estate in order to raise the product price. He wanted to ride the trend, that was his exact phrase."

I was starting to wonder where this was going. I had gone on a few winery tours before I left Ohio and this sounded like a variant of the local pitch, one that suggested it was rather chic to have skirted the law during Prohibition. Probably every other vineyard, distillery, and brewery that survived had done that in some way too.

"And I assume that this upgrade in image worked out for your father," I said.

"You're damned right it worked out. Now we have a string of gold medals printed across our label, along with the gecko-like creature that guards our vines from insect pests. He's our mascot, a cute little fellow named Jacopo. At home we call him Jake. But make no mistake, both of you, the bottom line is this: I will simply not allow a breath of scandal to sully that carefully polished image, one that has brought us all the way from Arturo Cavaletti going up and down the streets in Healdsburg with his donkey cart full of gallon wine bottles to being the winner at international competitions. The king of jug wines, as he then was known. Ha! Look at us now. No one will take that from us!"

She paused for breath on discovering that her hands had been kneading and twisting as she spoke and her cane was locked in her armpit. When she sat down again they gradually relaxed onto her lap.

"I quite understand," I said, wondering if I was starting to sound like Miss Rachel myself. "You don't want the words *murder* and *Cavaletti* to ever be used in the same sentence, at least in public."

"Now you do understand me, young man." She rose and held out her hands to us. "Have Rathbone, our valet, write you a check for a deposit on your way out. You'll find him in his office next to the vestibule at the base of that accursed staircase. He can also arrange appointments with any of the other family members or staff you might wish to speak with. I will await your report."

We said our goodbyes. I inspected the stairs carefully as we left. They were made of the common *cantera* limestone that is such a plentiful material for architectural trim, sculpture, and pavements here. I didn't count them, but it was easy to believe the steps stretched for two tall stories without a break or pause for breath. The leading edges of the treads were rounded over, of course, but they were not carpeted. A thick rug with a pad under it would probably have saved Sebastian Cavaletti's life. No trace of the accident remained as far as I could see. The curious thing was that there was no handrail on either side. Older people, or those unsteady or short of breath for whatever reason, might have trouble navigating in either direction. That explained the elevators.

As we reached the vestibule at the bottom a tall angular man stepped out to meet us. He had also let us in and escorted us up the long staircase to the great room, but he had not introduced himself then.

"I am Rathbone," he said. Not offering to shake hands, in his left hand he held a small leather folder. "What is the amount of the deposit today, please?"

"Two thousand dollars," Maya said. That was our standard retainer at the start of a case.

Rathbone opened the folder and chose one of several checks inside. He had been prepared. It made me think Miss Rachel didn't discuss money with him in any detail. "And this is also for you, I was told." He handed us a folded sheet of paper. It contained the names and contact information for all of the family members present and the local staff.

Once we were out in the parking area Maya and I turned to look back at the house. I couldn't see Miss Rachel peering out the window at us. Of course, there were so many to choose from I couldn't scan them all. From that angle the façade was three stories of rustic but closely fitted stone. Sprays of ivy softened the look for about half of it.

"I wonder how deeply she's mourning poor Sebastian," Maya said, turning to face me. She had worn her business clothes for this visit; dark gray slacks and a white shirt with no jewelry. She had started putting her hair up lately for meetings like this, although usually it fell an inch or two below her shoulders. She had recently turned thirty.

"And I wonder," I said, "how much she's ever going to show us her feelings? Maybe there's a family tradition of being tougher than the disasters around you. Some families are held together more by business than by blood." I realized I hadn't been able to read Miss Rachel that well.

"Or perhaps at her age death is always at your shoulder, and the passing of a family member is not so shocking. Maybe she even felt slightly triumphant at having survived someone twenty years younger. Is she eighty?"

"She must be something like that," I said. "You don't think you're being harsh?"

"No. It must be a pleasant surprise at that age when you hear the bell tolling and it isn't for you."

"Been reading Hemingway again?"

"Not recently, but I still remember," she said. "Who's on the list?"

I surveyed the paper Rathbone had given us with the names of all the residents and employees of the household.

"We've got Miss Rachel, of course, and Elizabeth, the recent widow. Then the two kids, Luca and Rocco. Luca is thirty and Rocco's twenty-seven. Then there's Celeste Howard, Sebastian Cavaletti's secretary."

"And Rathbone himself."

"Right. He is the Cavaletti family representative among the existing household staff, which totals seven fulltime. Luis and Carmela live here. Luis is the gardener and Carmela is chief housekeeper. Then four other housekeepers and cooks, plus a driver."

"Who talks to the staff?" she said. "I speak the best Spanish."

"Let's have Cody start with Rathbone. He's got the common touch and his English isn't too bad."

CHAPTER TWO
CODY WILLIAMS

In his thirty-year history of interrogations on the Peoria Homicide Task Force Cody Williams had learned to prefer wealthy suspects to poor ones. They tended to have less of a chip on their shoulder since they never believed that Cody, as a cop, was remotely their equal. This made them vulnerable to his entire bag of tricks, since he knew they would underestimate him at every step.

Butlers or valets in service to such people required a more complex approach, to confront a blend of the prejudice and blindness of both rich and poor. On that brilliant morning, driving out to the Cavaletti rental estate on the northeastern edge of San Miguel, Cody knew his task was to somehow win Rathbone over to his side, an unlikely position that he could not yet have defined for himself.

At the entrance, a break in the fifteen-foot stone wall, he drove through a gate that opened for him after a twenty-second pause. He saw no one in the gatehouse, but small cameras scanned his Ford from two angles as he waited, so he assumed it was automated and he'd been cleared from within the house. This may have been Rathbone waiting for him. The lane was neatly paved in fitted stone and gradually curved for about fifty meters on the way up the slope. Tucked into a lush, overgrown ravine, the house had not been visible from the gate. He parked outside the triple tuck-under garage, partly concealed at the side of the structure, and walked a few steps back to take in an enormous house in rustic stone dominating an isolated setting. Half a dozen other widely separated homes were visible across from where he stood, but all were on hillsides beyond a steep wooded canyon. None seemed approachable on foot without going back out the gate to the road. He rang the doorbell.

A tall angular man with iron-gray hair and a widow's peak answered. He might have been in his late fifties. "I am Dennis Rathbone," he said. He was wearing a pair of gray flannel slacks with a perfect crease, and a matching vest over a starched white shirt. Cody tried to avoid the glare coming off his shoes.

"Cody Williams, of the Paul Zacher Agency." He handed Rathbone a business card but they did not shake hands.

"Please come in." With a measured pace Rathbone led him around the left side of the staircase into an office. It bordered a pair of elevators.

Cody guessed Rathbone's height to be about six-foot-one, so he had two inches on the butler. But where Rathbone was slim, Cody had broad shoulders and was still well muscled at sixty-three.

He found himself in a small windowless space that was nonetheless furnished with well-made but still rustic Mexican style furniture. The single example of art was a primitive but charming folk painting that looked like it might have come from Central America. On the wall opposite the desk a framed corkboard offered the schedule of the household personnel. Rathbone faced him with a patient look.

"You find yourself in charge of a small staff here," Cody said, pulling out his notebook. "Perhaps that's much the same as when you're at home." He watched Rathbone's face as he spoke. The man was fully relaxed, not feigning it.

"Well, yes, I suppose. Miss Rachel has asked me to explain our arrangements here. We have Luis and Carmela in charge. He's the gardener and she's the head housekeeper. They live in the quarters for married staff on the top floor in back. The others are also full time but they don't live on the property. So among them we have Carlos the driver and general helper; Maria the cook; her assistant, Ximena; and two maids; Lupe and Armida."

Cody checked these off against the list Rathbone

had given Paul and Maya. "A total of seven. Do they all answer to you during your tenancy here?"

"Yes, to me, but indirectly through Carmela, and to the property manager as well."

"What kind of group is it?"

"I'm not sure what you mean, sir." His face showed no expression.

Cody smiled and made a broad, open-handed gesture. "Does it function well? Do the members get along OK? Groups like this have an internal dynamic, a tone, I've found, in other cases. Each one is unique."

Cody had no experience at all in interrogating a group of seven household staff-members, but he knew something about small group interaction in general.

Rathbone settled back in his chair and folded his arms. "Well, if I may speak freely, I think that for my taste the tone among them is a bit too emotional, in ways that we wouldn't tolerate at home. But that's México, and the people here are different, so you are bound to see a different style of interaction. At the vineyard residence we would not permit, for example, all the chatter that goes on as people work inside this house. Naturally it stops when one of the guests comes within earshot, but I prefer that the staff work silently at all times, confining their conversation to communications directly related to the task. They should properly limit their socializing to after hours."

"I can see that. I suppose they mostly talk about family?"

"Often enough, although I usually make a point not to listen to it. I do have some Spanish, of course, from living in California."

"So you don't hear the gossipy side of it?"

"Not at all." He raised his shoulders and his eyebrows half an inch.

"Any romances here? I see that other than Luis and Carmela, who are married, there's Carlos, the only male among the four other women. Is he married?"

Rathbone's face was unexpressive. "No, I don't believe so, but I'm not altogether sure."

Cody could see from the slight tightening along his jaw that there was another level to this question that Rathbone wished to avoid. Given his position of authority and trust with the Cavalettis, Cody didn't expect much more than basic information from him. He moved the staff list across the desk toward the butler and rotated it to face him. "Could you put down the approximate ages of everyone on the staff here after their names? As close as you know them." He watched Rathbone as he did this, but the man displayed no hesitation as he finished and handed the paper back to Cody.

"I see that Ximena, the cook's assistant, is twenty and Carlos the driver is twenty-three. Is anything happening between them?"

Rathbone made a brief dismissive gesture; his hand lifted from the desk as far as his wrist. "The usual flirting behavior I suppose. They're both good-looking and healthy young people. Uneducated, of course, and rather common, but nonetheless, I think it's about what you would expect in close quarters like this."

"Of course. During the evening when Sebastian Cavaletti died did you admit any visitors?"

"No, but I was not in place here for the entire time between dinner and the discovery of Mr. Cavaletti's body. I had some other personal business to attend to and it may have happened that someone was let in either by Mr. Cavaletti himself or someone else in the household. I can say that as far as I was told, no one was expected. Usually if they know someone is coming they will inform me."

"You didn't hear the bell ring?"

"No, but again, I was not always in a position to hear it. I was in my room on my laptop after 9:45."

"But I assume in that case we could see any comings and goings on the camera tapes from down at the gate."

Here Rathbone displayed an uncomfortable look. "Unfortunately the system here, as I was told by the house manager, is programmed to overwrite the prior day's recording when it starts the following morning at five A.M. It stores nothing long-term. At this moment the system would have everything from that time this morning, so only about four hours."

Cody frowned. This seemed both frivolous and careless for a security system, but it had not been Rathbone who set it up that way. He wondered whether the tape was programed to provide no long term records of what went on among the tenants. Grand houses like this might have a variety of uses for those who could afford to rent them. The only chance to retrieve anything would've been when Delgado arrived before midnight on the evening of Sebastian Cavaletti's death, and during the search that followed. Cody let the idea go.

"How would I go about having a conversation with some of these staff people without being too disruptive? Would you be able to set that up for me?"

"Yes. Tell me what you wish and I'll have Carmela arrange it."

"Excellent. I'd like to start with Ximena, the kitchen helper, if I may. Maybe tomorrow afternoon at her convenience? I don't want to interfere with lunch clean up."

"Of course. Let us say at three o'clock tomorow."

Cody rose to leave, folding the personnel list and putting it in his shirt pocket. Rathbone got up and they walked out into the vestibule. His voice dropped a notch in volume as he glanced up the stairs. No one was in view. "Permit me to say one more thing, Mr. Williams.

I'm sure you know your business very well. But if Miss Rachel has hired the Paul Zacher Agency to establish that the death of Mr. Cavaletti was a tragic accident, then you may very well rely on that to be the case. To do otherwise would be a waste of time. Until tomorrow, then." He finished with a curt goodbye nod.

And that was the first line of defense, Cody thought as he got into his car and backed away from the garage, and not so bad, either. Dennis Rathbone had a natural manner both of authority and of being well in-formed. Of course, that part about Sebastian Cavaletti's death being an accident might even turn out to be true. Although he had found nothing hinky (a favorite cop word of his) about the situation so far, Cody's instincts were telling him that something was still not quite right. Maybe it was nothing more than the Agency being hired to prove that there was nothing wrong.

CHAPTER THREE

Maya and I noticed Cody's car parked near the garage as we drove up at about nine-fifteen. Carmela answered the door and took us up the stairs for my meeting with Celeste, Sebastian Cavaletti's private secretary. Maya waited for her return in the great room to begin her interview with the new widow, Elizabeth Cavaletti, who apparently lived in seclusion for health reasons.

I had chosen Celeste to complement the start-with-the-staff theme that Cody recommended. In his experience, the staff, he remarked, would often try to protect the family, but they weren't always certain how to do that, since the family tended to shield them from what was really going on. At least to the degree that was possible. This made sense to me. Celeste, as the personal secretary to the late Sebastian Cavaletti, would have occupied both a loftier and a more connected position than any of the others that came with the house. She would know at least part of his game, and possibly more than

Cavaletti had thought she knew. While Rathbone could monitor the comings and goings of the family, Celeste was in a position to peer into the inner workings of the vineyard business at the highest level.

I waited for her outside on a small terrace that overlooked the rising slope across the wooded ravine. Every house, and there weren't many, looked huge and expensive, screened from its immediate neighbors by terrain and foliage. The views over San Miguel and the surrounding mountains would all be as pricey as they were long. The secluded retreat where I stood was attached to a book-lined sitting room. It offered a sense of privacy and calm that the larger and more public areas of the house did not. Set in an arc, three deep and comfortable chairs with small tables between them faced the view. The plants were scaled correctly and placed to provide atmosphere and character, but not interfere with the kind of intimate conversation I was hoping for from Celeste.

She would probably be a woman who was older and quite businesslike, I thought, perhaps even reticent about talking to me, as both a stranger and an investigator in a time of great emotional turbulence caused by a sudden tragedy. Cavaletti Vineyards was an important grower in the California wine country. I had researched them online to prepare for this meeting, and they were one of the biggest producers in Sonoma County. I wondered how much I'd be able to get out of her. I always tried to find some small point to connect with to establish a link between us as we started like this. My painter's eye was often an aid in finding such a detail. Was she, for example, wearing a small gemstone in a pendant that I could identify and mention? Or from her accent, did we both come originally from the Midwest? Beyond that, I made no assumptions. I can always rely on improvisation, and my portrait painting experience rarely fails me in sizing people up. Most faces can be read like a landscape, and when they are too veiled to offer that, then that disguise in itself provides information.

I've also done more witness and suspect interviews than I can count, but I was still not prepared for Celeste as she stepped out onto the terrace. Before I could fully take in her appearance, her grip nearly shattered my fingers when we shook hands.

"Be careful," I said with a grimace. "My trigger finger was in there somewhere. Not sure I can find it now." I felt like I had lost control of the conversation right out of the gate.

"I'm sorry. Sometimes I don't know my own strength." She gave me a blazing smile that nearly made me forget the pain, but not quite. I also knew that references to unconscious strength are often a veiled warning of a further battering to come.

An unlikely aggressor, Celeste Howard was about five-foot six, with a blond pixie haircut. For this meeting her round face was unshaded by subterfuge or shadow, offering huge luminous brown eyes and perfectly inviting lips. Her graceful figure did not suggest a powerful, bone crushing physique. Without being delicate, she was extremely feminine. I placed her age at about twenty-seven, and not a single thing about her suggested she was not fully in possession of herself and her personal goals.

To stop staring into her face I glanced down at my list, although I already knew what it said. "I see here that you were Sebastian Cavaletti's secretary."

She nodded. "And his masseuse. Being his private secretary wasn't exactly a full time job. He had a roomful of clerks at home for the routine parts of the business."

"Why don't we sit down?" I thought for a moment about that combination of duties, wondering how many hours a day being his masseuse could add to it. Looking at how she was dressed, I tried not to think of it as fleshing out her schedule.

For this conversation Celeste was wearing the briefest of turquoise linen shorts with tiny frivolous cuffs and a white close-fitting tank top made from a lightly ribbed fabric that defined her contours exquisitely. Still, her impression was not all sugar and spice. I looked at her again for a long moment, discovering an element in her manner that made me feel a degree or two off balance, even more than my hand injury would explain. It seemed prudent to avoid touching her again, and I was now planning to.

"I was very sorry to hear about Mr. Cavaletti's death," I said.

"Thank you."

I don't ever try to categorize people, to put them in boxes or label them, because it interferes with truly seeing them. But there was something about Celeste that made even the idea of labeling her impossible. Sensing that she might be more willing to talk than her privileged position suggested, I decided to be more direct with her than I would otherwise, even slightly aggressive. I could always rein that in if it didn't work, but while she might well have been light on her feet, she didn't appear to want to dance around the issues.

"Is Miss Rachel planning to keep you on for a while? Or has she said?"

"Yes. She's asked me to stay on long enough to help put Sebastian's affairs in order."

"How many was he having?"

Celeste didn't blink as she regarded me carefully. "Only one that I knew of for certain. Maybe I'll unearth some others in his correspondence. You can never tell until you take a closer look, can you?"

"Would that be correspondence you didn't help him with?"

She folded her hands in her lap and smiled patiently as if she was finding me not quite as bright as she'd expected. I didn't mind that because it was helpful when people underestimated me. "Sebastian was a militant computer illiterate by choice. He didn't even own a cell phone. It was a matter of principle to him not to enter the twenty-first century if he could advance his cause some other way. Part of my job was to facilitate that."

"OK, I can see that. Some people prefer to remain behind while time marches on. It may be a matter of personal taste, but I didn't think the last century went all that well, either. Maybe some of the music was pretty good, and the painting in the first part. I'll give you that, at least."

"I don't remember very much of it. Anyway, there might be some handwritten letters in his files I haven't seen. I've only been with him for a little over three years."

I leaned closer to her. "That intentional withdrawal from technology must've been quite a handicap for a businessman."

"Not if he had the right kind of help at his side." Here came the smile again that suggested I wasn't going to get the best of her. I cranked up my game another notch.

"And you made sure he did."

She shrugged and then nodded. "That was my job. Being technologically aloof was his way of being above everything he didn't wish to bother with. Sebastian was focused on the grapes, the weather, the ongoing need to sample everything as it matured. He saw himself as an old fashioned Italian craftsman. For the rest he often relied on me, and I'm very good at what I do, Paul. Can I call you Paul, by the way?" Her voice grew softer on that last sentence, although it stopped well short of an outright caress.

"Everyone calls me Paul." I leaned forward even more, and with a confidential air. "So by now you must know all the Cavaletti family secrets."

She nodded slowly, looking me directly in the eye. "Yes, I do." Her mouth remained slightly open as if she was planning to bite me.

As I moved within inches of her face, my voice dropped to a whisper. "I think you're one of those family secrets." When she held my gaze steadily, but without responding to this, a minuscule satisfied smile shaped her lips. I pulled back and went on. "Did Sebastian have an abnormal gait, or any other physical problems, say with balance or equilibrium?"

"None that I couldn't help him get over. He was doing fine until the day he died. He didn't ever miss a step."

Still, he missed two flights of them, I thought, but without saying so. "He must've needed a lot of bodywork to maintain that kind of vigor. I was told he was close to sixty."

She pulled the left spaghetti strap of her tank top

a half-inch closer to her neck, a gesture that made me scan the surrounding skin in detail. I could find nothing wrong with it.

"Look, it kept him from tightening up after a tough day among the vines. I could make him relax and forget about the ongoing conflicts with Miss Rachel and his flaky wife. He was a hands-on manager and he loved my touch, as anyone would."

I could see a variety of ways to respond to this, but I avoided all of them, massaging my hand instead. Perhaps her touch had gotten me off on the wrong foot with her. "Do you know what's wrong with Elizabeth? I keep hearing about her isolation, although I know she came along."

"Sure. It's no secret in this house. Elizabeth is a ruthless hypochondriac. She's used that to manipulate people her entire life. Sebastian always called her B.C."

"Which stands for what? Was she that much older than he was?" I knew Maya must be with her at that moment, but I hadn't met her yet.

"No. It stands for Basket Case. To him she was never Liz after the first year or two of their marriage."

"Did you ever give her any bodywork?"

"Not even with a stick." She looked out over the ravine as if searching for more meaningful topics.

"So you two didn't get along."

"We didn't connect much, and that was easy

enough. Elizabeth was jealous of my relationship with her husband because she didn't have one. That was not a situation I created when I came aboard. Being his companion and private secretary was an open position I simply filled after an exhaustive interview. Sebastian has always had a private secretary."

"Has he always had a companion?"

"I never asked him that, but I always assumed he has."

I studied her for a moment. "Why are you being so frank? You don't know me."

A compact shrug of her bare shoulders followed, a substandard one for México, where the shrug is one of the principal forms of creative expression, ranking in importance right after painting, sculpture, and ballet, to which it is distantly, if unofficially, related.

"I don't know any other way to act. I'm usually not charming unless there's a reason to be. Besides, with Sebastian gone now, no one but me will tell the truth here anymore. What else do you want to know?"

"Are you in Sebastian's will?"

Standing up with a cryptic look, Celeste folded her arms and stepped away from me, considering this as she placed most of her weight on one leg and gazed out over the parapet into the deep green valley, chaotic with palms and yuccas. I couldn't believe it was the first time the idea had crossed her mind. In that posture her body was perfectly articulated, her thighs and butt, her lower back and calves smoothly muscled. She almost looked more animal than human. Without appearing to be a workout fanatic, there didn't seem to be a superfluous ounce on her. In a way I could say about few other people I've known, everything about her body seemed *necessary*, almost inevitable, both to her and to anyone who looked at her. This also told me something about Sebastian. I could now believe he was in a number of ways a connoisseur. It wasn't only about the grapes.

"I'll find out about the will soon enough, won't I?" she said.

I had forgotten about it already. His estate wasn't paying my bills. "I'm surprised that you haven't seen it." Surely she would know where it was kept. "You must be deeply saddened by his loss."

"Believe it, Paul, I'm crushed, no pun intended. Soon I'll be out on my own again. I'll never find another job this good, one that uses my whole range of talents. It's tragic to peak so young; I feel like a sixteen-year-old Hungarian gymnast when the Olympic medals stop coming in. Now it's all about what happens next, and I just don't know what that's going to be."

I shook my head and smiled at her. "Celeste, I'm sure there are many good times ahead for a person like you." I had absolutely no doubt about this.

"Yes, but they won't pay me nearly as well. Partying is a different issue. I know how to party, and I can do it on a budget. It doesn't always have to be like this."

"I'm sure. Is it possible that Sebastian's death was a murder dressed up as an accident?" This was to steer her back on course.

A trace of weariness came into her voice. "Paul, I don't know every single thing that goes on here. Why would you think that? Sebastian often had a few drinks in the evening. You can't be surprised if he liked his wine. He was perfectly capable of falling down those steps without anybody's help. At home in Sonoma County his house was huge, probably as big as this one in square feet, but it was nowhere taller than a single story. He wasn't used to multiple floor levels. None of us were."

Yet it wasn't Miss Rachel who cartwheeled down the stairs, despite her age and cane. "Did anyone hate Sebastian?"

"In the wine business?"

"Was that a multiple choice question?"

"I think a few people might have. It's a group where everyone has known each other since nursery school, with all those buried family rivalries. While on the surface it's now mostly kissy face greetings, and there's a big shared tasting room in town, there are still some rude feelings at a deeper level. Not everyone appreciates the fact that his father was able to raise the reputation of Cavaletti Vineyards way above the jug wine level, and then acquire some other premium labels as well. Some felt he should've stayed down there where he started out. The Cavalettis were never part of the original vintner royalty, you know? A few of the seven founding families felt, well, somewhat *overtaken* by his marketing efforts. He was simply very good at it." Celeste looked at me and pursed her lips, as if to say, kiss, kiss, as one vintner to another. I could well imagine her at those wine country parties. What an asset for Cavaletti Vineyards!

"The ones that didn't like him were the people who started out classy, who didn't have to raise their brand image up by the bootstraps," I said. "They probably thought the Cavalettis were climbers."

"That's exactly right."

"What about his position within the family?"

"Well, he and Miss Rachel would've never gotten along if they hadn't had the same goals and the same business heritage to protect. It was often a chilly atmosphere between them, but I always thought that was all right. Why mix family feelings with business? It's better not to connect that way. I don't believe in complicating things." She paused for a moment with the air of someone about to utter an important truth. "You'll find that my needs are quite simple."

I found no reason not to take her word for that. "Does Cavaletti Vineyards make money?"

She gestured broadly toward the luxury surroundings with both hands. "Does this place look like a no-tell motel where we're shacked up for a month of nooners? Cavaletti Vineyards makes money by the carload. We all flew down in the family jet. It's still parked at the León Airport while the local staff polishes the tires every day."

"Was Sebastian a gambler?"

She chuckled. "Not after Elizabeth started staying in her own room all day. He had the run of the house twenty-four seven. It has eight bedrooms, plus four in the guesthouse."

"What about the kids? Luca is thirty and Rocco is twenty-seven. They're around your age and I know they've come along on this visit too, although I haven't talked to them yet."

A look of careful indifference came over Celeste's face. "They're about what you would expect; a couple of boys spoiled from birth waiting their turn behind the wheel of the old Bentley, OK? Just like Sebastian did while his dad went month after month without dying. He was forty-five when the old man finally passed."

"Was he in good shape until the end?"

"What Sebastian told me was that his father was badly weakened by a stroke for the last three years of his life, and although he was aware of things around him and could still speak fairly well, he was partially paralyzed, and he was angry about his disabilities. Miss

Rachel ran the show without always keeping him informed. Sebastian had to fight to get his share of control back when his dad died. Their first big battle was over planning the funeral. She lost, and that set the precedent for what followed. Now her role is to be the dowager queen, struggling to maintain even a fraction of her influence behind the throne. It's an old story, and for me, a very boring one. I'm like, give it a rest, OK? Go buy a place in Scottsdale."

"Who are her allies within the household?"

"I think Dennis Rathbone may be the only one, although he's his own man first. You'll find he leaves his mark on things, subtly, of course. Certainly not Sebastian or Elizabeth. The boys are polite but not close to her."

"You seem to know a great deal about the family." I tried to say this with a smile.

"People tell me things. I guess my transparent sincerity must inspire confidence, so people like to get close to me, you know?"

"Are you saying people would like to have a piece of you?"

She didn't answer for a moment, looking over the densely green narrow valley toward the grand houses across the way. Then she faced me. "I would have to say that not everyone does, but some clearly do. You do, for example, *Paul*." Her eyebrows went up, forming a kind of question mark.

I couldn't stop looking at her flawless mouth, even if I was often startled by what came out of it. "I only want to hear what you think. I'm a curious guy, and you seem like the ultimate insider to me."

"Believe it. There are things I could tell you that no one else can. I could deliver this case for you. Maybe I will. I could place it like a present right in your lap." She made a gesture of dropping a handkerchief with two fingers.

"Go ahead. I'm listening." I couldn't help but smile at this image.

"Then we'll talk about it again later." Both her index finger and her upward look pointed subtly to the parapet on the terrace overhead.

Celeste turned and I watched her walk back into the house. I was again rubbing my injured hand. When the door closed behind her with a subtle click I thought I heard some movement on the floor above, perhaps the slight scraping of a steel chair on the tile, but taking two steps backward to the rail and looking up, I couldn't see anyone and I heard nothing more. After making a few notes of some of the details of the conversation I went back inside. I wasn't likely to forget the main points.

CHAPTER FOUR
MAYA SANCHEZ

Although Maya had driven out to the rental estate with Paul, she didn't know where he went after they separated, other than for a conversation with Celeste. When Carmela returned and showed her the way to Elizabeth's bedroom, Maya knocked softly on the door. It was the master suite, leading down a short, unobtrusive corridor off the pool table end of the great room. The door felt massive and unyielding under her hand. The house was full of period elements, some of them hundreds of years old.

She knocked again, harder, on the weathered surface. A faint voice, almost like a whine, responded from within. Without clearly understanding what was said, Maya pushed the door open, hearing the antique hinges grind slightly. It would be impossible to sneak up on Elizabeth unless she was sound asleep, she thought. Similarly, people in the great room would hear her coming out. Didn't that work both ways?

The walls inside were painted a pale blue with a subtle touch of green, not a sentimental sky blue kind of color, but one that spoke of nuance and sophistication. A bronze four-poster bed under a domed exposed brick ceiling, a *bóveda*, as they are called, dominated the room. Opposite, a wall of French doors revealed a comfortably furnished terrace and broad views to the west. Out there unmoving on a wicker settee, a woman looked off over the city, her arms folded as if patiently on call. Next to her was a waiting wheelchair.

To the left, an open door led to a sitting room and an elaborately tiled bathroom beyond. Leaning back against three layers of pillows on the bed was a woman wearing a salmon-colored silk robe over a white cotton nightgown. Her hair was loose and unruly with a violent inch-wide shock of white running through the dark brown from her center part over the left side of her head. Nodding in weary welcome, she gestured Maya to approach.

"I want to thank you so much for coming to visit me. It's very hard for me to get up these days. Since my illness, I can rarely even manage to dress anymore, as you can plainly see." She held up both hands as if to suggest that the informality of the robe was not her fault. "If it weren't for Elena out there I don't know how I'd manage at all. Please have a seat."

Maya pulled a delicate side chair up to the edge

of the bed near the footboard and sat down.

"You must be one of those people from the detective agency, is that right? Miss Rachel sent Carmela to tell me you'd be coming today. She didn't want to bother me herself." Elizabeth's voice was thin and wheezy, requiring her to store up a measure of breath between sentences. "Everyone has been so wonderfully kind here, with this terrible tragedy that we've had. I simply don't know how we can go on without Sebastian." She pulled a lacy handkerchief from her sleeve and pressed it lightly to her eyes. Her chin quivered like a small animal. "He was like a rock, a foundation under all of us, in good times or bad. Of course, this altitude isn't helping me any now either."

"I'm so sorry to disturb you at a time like this. I'm Maya Sanchez from the Paul Zacher Agency."

"That's right. I know I heard that name. They do tell me a few things now and then."

Elizabeth Cavaletti's face became slack and expressionless. Subtle jowls had extended her jaw line to frame the upper part of her neck. They gave her lower face a mournful canine expression. Her rimless glasses magnified the pale watery vagueness of her eyes, and her dead-white skin offered no sense of having a future.

"How are you doing with all this? It must be the most terrible shock, and so unexpected," Maya said. Although she guessed that Elizabeth was in her mid to late fifties, her face appeared to be the victim of a progressive decay, as if it were approaching the point of dissolving into a degree of shapelessness that would be hard to read as human. From its extreme paleness, that might have come more from mold than advancing age.

The bedridden woman shuddered slightly and tried to pull herself together with a long sigh. "It's nothing new for me, of course. I must tell you that in my life I have been no stranger to pain and suffering. I've lived with it since shortly after my marriage to my dear Sebastian thirty-two years ago. Now he's gone so soon, and I shall deeply miss his constant attentions and kindnesses to me. His unfailing concern. No one could ever replace him. I'm sure I shall never marry again, even when this cruel mourning period has passed."

Maya couldn't prevent her eyebrows from lifting at the thought. Would Elizabeth require gurney service going down the aisle? Would they sing "Here rolls the bride?"

As Elizabeth covered her face with both hands her sleeves slid back to display the sagging flesh along her arms, like long sausages strung from a clothesline. "I feel like I shall go on in a state of mourning much like Queen Victoria did for her poor Prince Albert, when after forty long years of unrelenting pain…"

"Are you satisfied that Mr. Cavaletti was still quite steady on his feet recently? I understand we've been charged with proving that his fall on the stairs could only be accidental." Maya did not often interrupt people she was talking to, since that would not reflect Mexican manners, but it appeared she was going to need to carve herself a niche in this conversation to insert anything she might wish to say.

"Oh no, oh no." Elizabeth shook her head to a degree that for her might have been seen as robust, although in others only vague. "No, Sebastian was a most vigorous man, still in his prime, in fact. I only wish I could have been more of a, you know, a real *companion* for him. He was always so patient about that. I know he would never have glanced at another woman."

"And how could he?" Maya nodded slowly as she listened, already feeling she had somehow entered the world of a Mexican *telenovela*, or an American soap opera.

"Have you ever seen his picture? He always so reminded me of Ricardo Montalbán. Of course, Sebastian was Italian down to his socks, but he never minded hearing me say that about him, not that he ever thought of himself as a rake. If you haven't seen a photo of him, have Rathbone find one for you. We never travel without a few already signed to give away, and at home the house is full of them. Of course, I'm so glad to have them now. That's all I have left. I know I shall have to face Miss Rachel on my own from now on." Her face crumpled briefly but the moment passed.

Having already sampled the Miss Rachel style, here Maya attempted to picture Italian socks. Elegant certainly, and monogrammed in a Gothic script. Possibly by Gucci or Ermenegildo Zegna? But exactly what else did that mean? She knew very well how far beyond her native element she was now drifting, but she didn't care to show it. She watched Elizabeth for a while with a grave look, wondering how she could possibly redirect this conversation back to the real world. Any kind of reality would do, and she didn't feel she'd seen any yet.

"How were things within the household going?" Maya said, trying to inch toward more substance. "It must be very complicated to run a successful family business."

Elizabeth took this in thoughtfully, turning to pick up a glass of clear liquid on her bedside table and take a long sip from it. That's got to be gin or vodka, Maya thought. She'll call it cough medicine if I ask her. The woman hadn't been coughing at all.

"Since you ask, I suppose I can say that we are like a lot of people with money. We have no worries from the outside, of course, so our challenges have been mainly from within. Health problems, as you may not realize yet at your age, of course, can bring down that level of spontaneous joy, of camaraderie within a family, which is why I have always tried to put on a brave front, never truly voicing the degree of my pain and suffering. I believe I have succeeded so well in that. Who would ever guess?"

"You hold it in silently, bravely within yourself, and so well," said Maya, thinking she would have Paul make her a huge margarita later. In his version, he always blended lime and lemon juice to perfection.

Elizabeth gave her an almost startled look. "You understand me so well! How can that be?"

"Mexicans are sympathetic people by nature." She was wishing for her own glass of gin now, even though she preferred tequila.

"I guess that's true, Maya. We have eleven Mexicans on the vineyard staff at home, although we never use them inside the house. They're all legal, of course. But we prefer the British as being more reserved, you know, like Rathbone. He would never talk, even if he knew anything, which I don't think he does. About the family, I mean. Not that there's anything to know really."

"Of course. How are your boys taking this?" Maya was now wondering what it was that Rathbone might know. Being reserved was not the same as being blind.

"Well, as you have probably heard, Luca and Rocco both positively *worshiped* their father. What else can I say? He was both night and day to them."

"A true beacon unto their darkness," Maya said, nodding, with no idea where in her head this had come from other than that her growing desperation was pulling up things she would never otherwise say. "We haven't talked to them yet."

"Nor have I, except right after Sebastian's body was found. But I know that once you leave, they'll be up here weeping their eyes out just to help me get through one more day. That's all I ask. This is a family that is all about support, you know. Unlike many others I could mention back in Healdsburg."

"Am I holding them back from a visit?" Maya saw this as an opportunity.

"Possibly, and I'm starting to fade a little myself. Thank you for this chance to talk with you. You've been most kind."

As Maya rose, Elizabeth reached again for the glass at her side.

"We can take this up again when you feel you're ready for it," Maya said, returning the chair to the wall and turning toward the foot of the bed. Most of the wall opposite was covered by a long built in armoire. The door panels were all fronted by slender turned spindles backed with a blue fabric that matched the paint color. The effect reminded Maya of the screened confessional in a Catholic church, or in this case, a nunnery. It felt like isolation, a voluntary, even determined segregation from both the family and the outside world. Struggling to keep her pace to a normal speed, she found slipping out through the heavy door was far easier than entering. As she closed it softly on the ancient hinges she heard Elizabeth's voice call out in an amplified whine, "Elena! Elena? Come in here now! Where are you? I need you!"

A pressure she had not realized was there had lifted from her lungs. Feeling she could breathe freely again in the great room, Maya paused for a moment beside the ornate antique pool table. The balls were perfectly arranged, but the cue pointed nowhere. The walls were painted a dark red, with wormy seasoned woodwork that enhanced the feeling of age, although Maya knew the house was no more than fifteen years old. At the narrow end of the table a sculptured niche in the wall framed a ceramic memorial that displayed four tiers of martyred saints bearing the symbols of their tragic stories.

She felt that in talking with Elizabeth she had come up against a stone wall, one that at every point felt soft and yielding to the touch but was nonetheless impenetrable. What went on behind that schizophrenic façade? Had Elizabeth chosen to know nothing or did she know everything and only chosen not to let on? After several years of Agency business Maya had concluded that people can lie to themselves more effectively than they can lie to others, perhaps because they have more of a stake in the lie.

Behind her, a deeper niche with a half-circle top housed an elegantly framed colonial painting of St.

Christopher bearing the child Christ on his back against a white background. Below were mixed shelves of books and ceramic figures. Across the room a small bar alcove, ornately carved and paneled in the same wood, was furnished with every kind of drink she could imagine. Although probably, she thought, most of the gin might already be gone.

Descending those dangerous steps, Maya felt almost giddy, as if she had emerged from an alternative reality and was still trying to reorient herself. At the bottom she paused to talk with Rathbone to set up a conversation with Luis and Carmela, the resident staff, as well as the cook and the two maids. Cody had already suggested that, from the hints he picked up from Rathbone, that Carlos the driver and Ximena the kitchen helper ought to be interviewed separately.

CHAPTER FIVE

At the Zacher Agency conference at the house we shared on Quebrada later that day, Maya was spelling out her reaction. Spitting it out might be more accurate. We had gotten beyond the polite preliminaries.

"I am sure this is the sickest case we have *ever* had," she said, stopping just short of slapping the table. "That Elizabeth woman. I can't find the words to describe her in English." She came up with two archaic-sounding Spanish phrases I did not recognize, and I've lived in this town for eighteen years. The three of us were sitting out in our loggia. An open bottle of Chilean red and three glasses sat on a tray before us. Because they encouraged case analysis, they all qualified for a tax write off.

Cody made a damping gesture with both hands, as if to say, slow down. "At least it's a real case this time, not some pro bono charity gig again, and we're getting paid for it. Drawing a salary is always your big issue. Sometimes it's mine too."

"And you don't have to write the checks like I do."
She shrugged. In the Paul Zacher Agency trio Maya was the responsible one, the one with insight into Mexican culture and mores, Cody was the procedural maven, the one who knew how to do it by the book when we chose to, and the occasional muscle, since he had the height and mass. I, as the artist, was the one who saw things differently, whenever that worked, if it ever did. Sometimes it did, and there was nothing else like it then. But even when it produced a breakthrough perspective, I couldn't always sell it to the others.

I hadn't even brought up my conversation with Celeste, knowing how it would set Maya off. "But I don't think it really is the sickest case," I said. "Maybe I should go down the list of comparative degrees of illness over those other sixteen outings?"

"No, Jesus!" Cody waved his hand across the table as if to eliminate the unproductive debris of past cases. "So what have we got this time, Maya? You talked to the recent widow. Give us some detail on how she's taking her loss."

Maya nodded slowly, trying to find a place to begin. "She would be more a patient for you than a suspect for me, a real head case." She filled the glasses while she described Elizabeth's manner and condition in more detail. In his youth Cody had walked away from an advanced degree in clinical psychology to become a third-generation homicide detective.

"You didn't think she was acting that way partly because of Sebastian's recent death? It's been only two days. A death in the family usually brings up stuff you don't want to remember. Maybe she only recently took to her bed." Cody said, always capable of giving people a break in the early phases of a case, where we now were. Not as much later.

"To me," Maya said, "it looked more like the way she got up every morning. Interacting with it made me feel off balance, because I couldn't tell how much of it was real. It felt like a control trip, a system of getting her way among a set of other strong-willed people. There's a lot of guilt in it that she projects onto other individuals. Think of Miss Rachel and what it takes to oppose her. And we don't even know what Sebastian was like."

"Now we're starting to get a sense of what he had to deal with," said Cody, "and there's more of that coming."

"Sebastian was a man of cultivated tastes who preferred to live in the previous century more than this one," I said. "A master craftsman in making wine. I got that much from Celeste."

"Well, I've mostly lived back then, too," Cody said. "Nothing wrong with that. The pay was better."

"I'm talking about values now, more than calendar or salary levels," I said. "Celeste told me he refused to use a computer. He didn't have a cell phone. And I'm thinking that it was right around the turn of this century that Sebastian's dad died and he took over, maybe in 2001 or 2002? I'm not sure if that's at all connected."

"Who's left to talk to now?" said Maya, rubbing her hands together as if anyone else might be an improvement over Elizabeth.

Cody pulled the list out of his shirt pocket. "Most importantly, although we won't know for sure until we talk to them, we have the two sons, Luca and Rocco. I would guess those conversations would have to be set up through Miss Rachel, or possibly Rathbone. Then we have the staff, where only Celeste and Rathbone have talked to us so far. There are seven other full time employees that run the household, but they're not part of the family. They'll stay here when the Cavalettis go back to California."

"I've got the cook, the two housemaids, and Luis and Carmela lined up for later today," said Maya. "I left the driver and Ximena the kitchen helper for special treatment."

Cody was writing all this down.

"Let's talk about Celeste next," Maya said, giving me a firm look for no reason I could think of.

"Of course," I said, sensing quicksand nearby. I pulled out my compact notebook and opened it at random to a blank page. "Celeste is a modest and unassuming woman in her early nineties. One with no more than a seventh grade education, I would guess. While she walks with a pronounced limp, her hunched-over back doesn't seem to be the cause for that, so it must be a separate problem. Overall, I would say that her violent stutter and her thick Albanian accent still did not unduly impede our conversation. Similarly, the fact that her nose droops forward far enough to rest on her upper lip did not affect her articulation, and, luckily, she is aware of it and very quick with a tissue when it drips." Succinct and to the point, I thought, finishing with a modest grin. A slight silence followed this detailed contribution to the case file.

"Paul," Cody said with a dense overlay of calm. "Please. For once, this is an active case. People are paying us for our time. Let's respect their investment." Shaking his head, he rose and poured out the rest of the wine bottle into the three glasses, skimping noticeably on mine.

"I already heard a description of her from Carmela as she took me to Elizabeth's room," Maya said with a display of dignity and seriousness. "You scored another hottie in this case, didn't you, *mi amor cariño?*"

"OK, I may have been a degree or two off on my initial impression of her, but the light on the terrace wasn't that good."

"Did you take any notes?" Cody said, nearly throwing up his hands.

"A few. More than that I didn't have to."

"Spit it out, then," said Maya. This must have been a recent addition to her American slang lexicon, a favorite hobby of hers. "I'm surprised you didn't wear a wire."

"Frankly, I didn't know what I was going to be dealing with."

"Do you now?"

"I have thought about it since, briefly." Not that this answered her question.

"I'm sure, and more than once."

"OK, enough. I came away feeling that Celeste is a handful, and just because Sebastian is gone, she's not necessarily finished with the Cavalettis. She had a great position there with her very personal involvement with the deceased, and she's not going to walk away from that without something equivalent waiting for her. But is she a suspect? Maybe, but her situation was also badly damaged by his passing, so I have a hard time seeing any motive with her. I doubt that it was a crime of passion if she killed him; she seems too calculating for that. Anyway we don't know if it even is a murder."

"Just how close was she to Sebastian?" Cody said.

"I don't think you could've inserted a knitting needle between them."

"So who does have a motive?" Maya said. "It could be that Elizabeth does, if she realized the degree of Sebastian's involvement with Celeste. What is hard to see is how able she is. I think the degree of her physical strength and mobility is a closely guarded secret, and one that I can't see us being able to analyze very well because everyone avoided her."

"And it could be that Miss Rachel has a motive," Cody said. "She recovers some degree of control over the vineyard again."

"Right, but why does she want that?" I said. "Most people eighty years old would be happy to retire with a lot of money and not have the stress of being in business every day. All we have so far is Delgado's statement that this was a murder, or that it might have been. That could be no more than an early hunch."

At the end the meeting wound down into a more standard case review, one I thought we would never have had this early if we'd had either more information or fewer suspects. I hate to make lists, but there were so many possible murderers in the house that we couldn't function without one, jotting down little coded marks after people's names. Underlining comments, sometimes twice. I felt like I needed to start a huge painting just to pull me back into a more normal reality.

"I'd like to set up Ximena, the kitchen helper, tomorrow afternoon at three. Would you come along on that? I'm afraid I'll intimidate her." Cody said this to Maya. With his size, he could intimidate a lot of people, and that wasn't always helpful, although there were times when it clearly had been in the past.

"Of course. I'll have talked to most of the others by then."

That afternoon he left us earlier than usual. Maya went back to the mansion and I went back to painting and had a respectable session. When she returned at about six we ate some leftovers and drank a little more wine. She'd gotten little from her staff talks, even though she'd also been able to have a brief conversation with Elena, Elizabeth's personal assistant. Later, at sunset, although we had no reason to celebrate, Maya and I got down the holiday cognac from the upper shelf. Back in the loggia she lifted her glass to me.

"I still like you best," she said. "I hope you still like me best."

I grinned. "I do, because you are the best. No question about it."

"But you always look at the others. This time it's Celeste."

"Yes! That's how I know you're the best. I make a point of never acting from ignorance. You know what an acute observer I am."

Maya seemed to understand the strength of my attachment, and even offered me a chance to prove it later.

CHAPTER SIX

The following morning Maya went riding at Rancho Camarena, where reconnecting with Martina, her Lusitano mare, would offer a fundamental and satisfying connection that might offset some of the grubbier aspects of our case. At breakfast she'd still been muttering about Elizabeth.

Shortly afterward Cody and I were on our way to see Diego Delgado at his office, passing through the *jardín* at a couple minutes before ten. Near the bandstand we crossed paths with him on his way to work. We paused and shook hands. Greetings are more complicated with three people, but once we had worked our way through the standard run of exchanges on health, family and weather, we got started on the Cavaletti case.

It was as easy to settle back on a cast iron bench in the freshness of mid morning as it was to go up to his office in the old Presidencia across the street. There the fan over his desk was a stale joke; it had offered no more than a futile twitch for the past four years. Delgado sat between us.

"You are talking now to the *familia Cavaletti*," he began. He was wearing one of his normal brown suits, the only color he ever wore, although this one was a trifle darker than the others. Perhaps it was the most formal one he had. Certainly the elbows showed little wear.

"Well, you know they called us right away and now they have hired us," Cody said with a small shrug, as if this should be no problem among a group of closely working associates that went back to when we started the Agency. That was true enough.

"It will not be to assist me this time," Delgado said. "But I know this already." His face was neutral. His position as a prosecuting investigator required a balanced set of expectations.

"You could say that we're working for the defense on this one," I said. "We would still like to know why you believe this was a murder. Have you found some physical evidence?"

"Before you answer that, I want to stress," Cody added, "that based on what we've found, we have not made up our minds whether it's a murder or not. The information we've gathered is not enough to make that call. We've only agreed to look into it, and the clients are hoping we can prove it was an accident. We are planning, as always, to show what it really was, whatever that will turn out to be."

"Proving it an accident will be most difficult to do," said Delgado, even as he nodded at this. "I believe you will find it easier to prove it was a murder."

An elderly, poorly dressed woman with wrinkled skin the color of a dry tobacco leaf shuffled up to us carrying a dirty backpack on one shoulder. She held out her hand palm upright and Cody placed a five-peso coin in it. She looked about Miss Rachel's age, but that was the only point of similarity.

"I never give them anything," Delgado said, making a gesture of dismissal as he moved on. "They come here in the morning in cars and they are picked up in the late afternoon. It is far less sad than it looks, but yes, I do have some physical evidence. The Cavaletti skull x-rays are telling us an interesting story. It is not a perfectly clear story, do you understand, but what story ever is in this business? Still, it offers us something to think about, a few points to discuss among professionals. Please come up to my office for more of this conversation."

Once on the second floor he led us into the small conference room in the rear corner. A quite respectable Mac computer was waiting for us on the conference table. Clearly Delgado had access to digital x-rays. I knew that most of his other equipment was old enough to be collectible.

When he pulled up the Cavaletti file it gave us four detailed shots: anterior, posterior, and both lateral views of the skull. We all saw at once that the right lateral view showed no damage. The left lateral view showed three impacts on the upper part of that side, with one leading curve that came around to damage the outer rim of the orbit, the socket that held the eye. The front view showed nothing. The fractures were linear and ragged on the bone and I couldn't read the pattern of a weapon on them, if there had been one. It could easily have been no more than Sebastian's head repeatedly hitting the rounded over leading edges of the steps themselves that killed him.

"Massive cranial damage," Cody said, shaking his head. "Cavaletti could never have recovered from that. These multiple fractures would've brought on major brain swelling. He was going over and over down those stairs for two flights with his head slightly turned to the right. How was the body found?"

"There was a fractured humerus on the left side too, that told us a little more. And on the man's neck one vertebra was fractured. I am told it is called C3. On the bottom landing near the front door, his body was doubled up in a position impossible for a living person."

"Had it touched the front door at all?" I said. "I'm thinking about whether some of these marks could be from the hardware."

"No sign of that," said Delgado. "But even more, here is the biggest issue for me." He loosened his tie as we moved on to scan the x-ray of the posterior portion of the skull. It displayed yet another linear depression fracture, but this time with a slight branch moving off from it. Delgado pointed to an area along the bottom edge of the blow. "Could this be a hint of something that curved away from the main line of the impact? Perhaps it is not from a stair, I have been thinking, because none of the stair edges have anything turning off them like this. I have checked them all."

I moved in for a closer look. An additional ragged fracture line was beginning to radiate from the main rod shape, but because of the angle of impact it was only a hint. Cody put on his reading glasses and bent over it with a frown.

"Injuries like this never reflect the detail very well," he said, "but I can see it too. That's hard to read."

"Well, yes, so now you can compare those fracture lines with the impact injuries on the flesh."

Delgado gave us a sober grin that suggested we were about to confirm a minor triumph of his. He clicked on another set of images from the row across the bottom of the screen. The first was a photo of the left side of the head. It had been shaved clean of hair. There were the three linear impact injuries, now defined as graphic violet bruises on the skin. All three had a profile of a massively impacted centerline, framed by diminishing damage tapering outward along both edges.

"That's from the stone stair tread," Cody said. "I've seen that kind of impact trauma before."

"And now there is this for you to think about." With the air of a magician unveiling his next trick Delgado pulled up the posterior view of the head. That had been shaved as well, and the hair must've been longer. Where the skull x-ray in this view had shown the beginning of a curve almost like a finger coming off the main line of the impact, the scalp photo showed the rounded-over mark of the weapon, but narrower than the stair treads, and there was now the same curving branch coming off the main stem. There was a heavy bruise with not much blood, but with some tearing of the skin. None of us said anything for a moment.

From a drawer within the table he pulled out a square of orange-brown dried clay. It held the impression made by a straight rod tapering toward the end and with a curved hook-like shape coming off it.

"That's just a typical fireplace poker," Cody said.

"Exactly, and the radius and the beginning of the curve are both quite close to what we have observed on the scalp image. I understand that it is not a precise measurement, but all the same I hope you can see this now."

"How did you get this?" I said.

"As you know, we of the police had the house by our own for six hours. In the Hospital General, Esquivel x-rayed the body and also photographed the impact images *muy pronto*, right away. He called me and said that besides the stair markings we had a funny blow both on the skin and to the skull on the back of the head and I should look for weapons of impact in the house. I am sure that this mark is from the fireplace set in the great room, which is seven meters from the top of the staircase. I have the poker itself now already in the evidence locker. I don't think they will miss it in this weather."

"The killer might, if that's what it was used for," Cody said. "Any prints on it?"

Delgado nodded his head in disappointment. "Several dozens, but all smudged and overlapping. It is a mess beyond saving. Beyond evidence, even, for our forensics crew."

"How do you read the scene, then?" Cody said. Since we came in he had been all business. All the Mexican courtesies had fallen through the cracks.

"It could be that Señor Cavaletti is hit from behind with the poker and falls forward down the steps unconscious even before he hits the first one. That could be one way to read it, or he is pushed or stumbles by fate and his own bad balance, and once unconscious is hit at the bottom with the poker to make sure he dies."

"Did you find any alcohol in his blood?" I said.

Delgado frowned. "Yes, yes we did." His left hand lifted this idea out of consideration. "But small in a quantity, as he would have had from two glasses of wine, *mas o menos*, more or less. I don't think that was part of this story."

"So then, with all of this, what comes next?" Cody said, his hands on his hips. I could see him assembling his own investigative team in a squad room somewhere in Illinois twenty years ago.

Delgado stood up as if this was a fundamental question, which it was for us too. "As you see, patience and time, Señor Williams. As always, we will gather information from behind the scenes. In the meantime I have ordered the family jet plane to be grounded at the León Airport, and the immigration authorities have collected the Cavaletti passports and those of the staff that came with them, which were already held there in the customs. The entire party."

"So now do you think we have a conflict of interest between us?" Cody said.

"Well, yes, if you are hired to prove this was not a murder. After seeing this, what else do you think?"

"We only said Miss Rachel was hoping it wasn't a murder."

Delgado gave me an ironic look. "But I have talked to her too, perhaps even more than you have. She told me what to think, although I do not work for her. I will try not to imagine what she told to you."

Five minutes later Cody and I paused on the street

outside. While the sun seemed brighter on the detail of this case out there, it still didn't illuminate anything helpful to our position.

"This doesn't look good," he said, "for the accidental death scenario we're being paid to promote. On the murder side of the argument, I admit that I'm a little troubled that the poker handle wasn't wiped clean, but it could've been gripped inside a shirtsleeve or a handkerchief and that would smudge the existing prints without leaving any new ones. And think of all the times that house has been rented in the winter and the tenants used the fireplace. The killer might have thought that was a handy coincidence."

"Right. And here's another awkward piece of the puzzle that now seems like I should've brought up before. You haven't talked to her yet, but that back of the head impact profile could also reflect the shape of the distinctive cane Miss Rachel uses. For the handle it has the same rod shape with a smooth length of a branch curving off it near the top, all thickly clad in antique nickel. From my cabinetmaker days in college, I can easily believe it's made of ironwood, which she acknowledged, and it is dense and heavy. It would be strong and substantial enough to strike a damaging blow without fracturing the wood or marking the nickel. She's quite proud of it since it was a collector piece that came from Jack London's estate."

"Paul, you know we're not going back inside now and tell that to Delgado."

"No. But down the road we might have to, and that could then be a bigger problem than it looks like now. Anyway, suddenly we have two possible weapons to consider, not just one."

"I'm not sure that offers us any definitive way to name the killer, only the means. The cane might have been lying around in the great room when Miss Rachel went to bed. Does she use it all the time?" Cody said.

"Not when Maya and I talked to her. She leaned on it now and then, and sometimes used it as a pointer or to make a broad gesture."

"OK, now you can say she had the means. We can't speculate yet about opportunity. But then why would she want to kill her nephew? Where's the motive?" Cody said.

"I've thought about that. There's the argument that it would put her back in control of Cavaletti Vineyards, since Elizabeth would inherit Sebastian's forty percent interest, and Miss Rachel could easily control Elizabeth, who has never been in control of the business, to say nothing of her life, her emotions, or her marriage. You heard Maya's report on her. Elizabeth is so self-absorbed she's practically cross-eyed. But as I said yesterday, I don't like that idea much."

"On the other hand," Cody said, "Maya also

speculated that Elizabeth's long term hypochondria was a control trip designed to make her more competitive with Sebastian and Miss Rachel. She might still be in this longstanding game somehow."

"That could be too," I said. "I haven't met her yet. Miss Rachel is experienced in management because she ran the show on her own when her brother, Sebastian's father, was disabled for the last three years of his life, but that was more than a dozen years ago."

"And Celeste told you," said Cody, "that Sebastian's relationship with Miss Rachel was cool at best. How reliable is she, besides being reliably hot?"

"Celeste?"

"Yes."

"Well, she's an insider who's franker than she needs to be, which to me makes a statement."

"In my experience on the force, people who tell you too much are often guilty."

"Interesting. Still, she seems genuine, if a little complicated. She knows she's attractive and she's willing to work it with anyone who pays attention."

"Like you, for example," Cody said.

"Yes, but is she saying everything else she knows? Because she's fishing for male attention it doesn't mean she's lying. Not remotely. Who ever tells us everything? She may have a need to set herself apart from what else goes on at the Cavaletti Vineyards, especially now.

I might have to get to know her a bit better before I can say any more."

"And I'm sure you will. You get all the dirty jobs. But is Celeste really a suspect?"

I stopped and fed him one of his favorite cop lines. "Cody, at this stage of the game everyone's a suspect."

"Of course. Does she have an agenda of some kind?"

"Well, certainly she wants to stay in her cushy niche until she can connect with another employer who appreciates her talents, gives her some credit, and pays her well. We haven't talked to the boys yet, but between Elizabeth and Miss Rachel, I think Celeste is on the way out from her position at Cavaletti Vineyards."

He looked at me for a moment. "I'm so glad Maya does the Agency hiring now. Celeste would never get through the door."

Of course, in our entire history of sixteen prior cases we hadn't ever hired anyone, and that was not likely to change now.

CHAPTER SEVEN

There was no need for the Paul Zacher Agency to flip a coin to decide who would be charged with breaking the distressing news to Miss Rachel that her nephew's death had been a murder. Cody and Maya had a prior engagement with the kitchen helper, Ximena, for that same afternoon. If they believed I landed all the young hotties, now would be the time to rethink that as they looked her over themselves. My sense of Miss Rachel was that, like the courtroom scene in *A Few Good Men*, she couldn't handle the truth, and she felt perfectly free to assemble her own competing version of reality, one that in this case was designed to obliterate mine.

Furthermore, the force of her objections to our new findings could well be formidable. Thinking of that ironwood and metal cane, I resolved to stand nowhere near the stairway during this conversation. Overall I was developing the idea that the women in the Cavaletti family and its entourage tended to be somewhat thorny, even if in widely different ways.

But it wasn't only about Miss Rachel's need to protect the family's elevated legend from scandal. What about my mission to deliver the news that her cane handle was nearly a perfect match for the impact blow that had launched Sebastian down two steep flights of steps to his death?

As I rang the bell at two o'clock I found myself wishing she would dismiss us from this case. In our intake notes for any client the form offers an important block at the bottom of the page that's headed: *The Client's Objective*. I felt like going back to that space and entering the words, *Mission Impossible*, after deleting, *Prove Nephew's Death an Accident*. It was not that we were afraid of difficult cases. Those cases had all been difficult in their own way, but we preferred to take the doable ones, since even then the success rate was only something like two-thirds. This was why painting was more rewarding for me. I was successful there about ninety percent of the time.

As my fingertips rested on the glossy varnished surface of the door, waiting for Rathbone to admit me, I felt a sudden chill. The ambience of the house had grown cooler to the touch. Had something changed in our reaction to it as well? The door swung open on silent hinges. Rathbone nodded, regarding me with a distant politeness.

Was he now seeing us as a threat to the family?

"Miss Rachel awaits you upstairs, sir." The slightly stiff bow did not include an offer to support my arm on that dangerous ascent into her presence. With a nod at the bottom, he disappeared into the service area at the left.

I know I climbed sixty steps in all. At the top I felt that five dozen might be a key multiple of many things, but I wasn't sure that any of them applied to this case. It was more about mood than math; elements more sinister than symmetrical, and I couldn't climb all those treads without imagining Sebastian rolling head over heels past me. I paused and looked back down from the top. If Delgado was right, and the victim had been struck unconscious at the highest step, then Sebastian had never felt a thing.

As if anticipating a problem, Miss Rachel did not turn as I entered the great room. Facing the fireplace, she sat on the tufted yellow leather sofa with her back to me, her hair tightly drawn into a gray bun, and both hands resting on the top of that Jack London antique cane. To her it must have been reassuring in the way a pacifier is to a toddler. I stood there for a moment, unsure whether she had heard me enter the room.

"Do you have a report for me, young man? Please have a seat. I suppose that two and a half days is enough time for most people in your business to come up with something useful."

Her emphasis on *useful* suggested my report needed to go through a pre-existing filter of some kind. I came around the sofa and settled at her left in a red brocade chair. Across the room a painting of a pious St. Francis lifted his eyes to heaven in prayer. It's going to take more than that to make this meeting go well, I said to myself. Flanking the fireplace, two arched openings gave access onto another covered terrace, one ample enough to entertain a dinner party of a dozen.

"We have made some progress, I think, Miss Cavaletti. It may not be what you're hoping for, but, as always, we've been constrained by the facts of the case. Sometimes they can be inconvenient if you're anticipating a certain outcome."

At this her eyebrows lifted. "Still, I'm sure everything you've discovered is open to interpretation by professional people with broader and more experienced insight. Any lawyer will tell you that. I know mine would. We can always call in an expert, or more than one, until we get it right." The set of her jaw was firm, but she didn't look at me. I also sensed a slight weariness in her tone. Her last sentence added some weariness to mine. Recalling my thoughts on the way over, for a moment I considered how to respond.

"Let me suggest to you that in employing the Paul Zacher Agency, you already have several experts on the scene. I have seen the x-rays from Sebastian Cavaletti's head injuries, as well as the photos of the bruising to the scalp." I purposely omitted saying anything about Delgado being the source of them. "They were taken immediately upon his admittance to the Hospital General, right after he was declared dead. While I'm not a medical professional, I do have some experience with such images, and I also have a painter's eye, which counts for something."

"And all of these images confirmed that he fell down a flight of stairs, is that not what you found?"

"It is. That's not in dispute. They also show a severe impact injury to the back of his skull. All the other trauma occurred on his left side. The impressions on the scalp at the rear of the skull do not match the edge of the stair treads. There was no other hard surface of that shape on the stairway for him to connect with as he fell."

"You must have gotten this from the police. I can imagine what kind of ax they have to grind."

"Are you suggesting the x-rays and the photos were faked?"

Her hands gripped the head of the cane as if to prevent it from flying out of her grasp, possibly at my head. When Miss Rachel did not respond to this for a long moment, I went on. "Your nephew came to rest, as you may have seen, on a level tiled floor in the entry. The injury on the back of his head was made either by the weapon whose impact caused his fall, or it was administered after his fall to make sure he was dead. These are the only conclusions available for a reasonable person."

"Impossible. *Reasonable* is a flattering term that you may be using too much in your own favor." Her fingers were bone white where they gripped the cane.

"If you wish I can arrange a time for you to view the evidence yourself."

"That won't be necessary, thank you. I've seen my share of carnage in business."

I could've sat there for a while more as she continued to dodge and contradict my statements, but I'd had enough. "Miss Rachel, I can't alter reality for you, if that's a condition of continuing with this case. Perhaps the Paul Zacher Agency is not the best choice to be investigating your nephew's death. Someone else might prove to be more accommodating in his interpretation of the evidence in these events. In view of what I've seen, I can no longer try to prove this was not a murder. It would be a waste of my time and your money."

As I studied her face I could find little to read aside from the rigid set to her jaw, so I went on. "I would not be offended if you asked the Paul Zacher Agency to withdraw from this case. To me, the choice would either be that or to pursue this investigation no matter where it leads. That's all I can offer you. We'd be happy to refund the unspent portion of your retainer."

Her mouth began to puff like a fish in an aquarium. "But your detective agency is the only one in this town, young man. Surely you're aware of that. You have no competition so you act as if you're free to do exactly as you please. A travesty like this is the result." She made a dismissive gesture with one hand as if that were how she imagined me doing it in betraying her family.

"I know. I'm sure you won't agree, but just as I can see only one agency, there is also only one reality to this case. A successful resolution requires that we all allow ourselves to face it."

Miss Rachel stared at the floor as her face slowly lost its stony edge. She pursed her lips as if she were trying to loosen something stuck behind her upper front teeth. I felt a momentary sympathy toward her. But on the other hand, I'd had too much experience with clients and suspects who could not accommodate reality, people who preferred to ignore it or beat their heads against it with no concern for reason. The case we'd recently finished, one we filed as *The Jericho Journals*, was a perfect example.

Miss Rachel looked into my eyes for the first time. "Don't walk away from me on this, OK, Mr. Zacher? I have no one left in this barbaric country that I can trust, and you would leave me in an untenable position. I can't believe you'd want to do that."

"But why trust me? You cannot depend on me to

shape the outcome for you. I want to be very clear about that. That has never been what we delivered. I can give you the name of a local public relations firm if you wish. That's not what we do."

Her gesture swept this from the room. "Then at least I can trust you to tell me the truth no matter what I would prefer to hear. Although that much is a poor second choice, it's still something rare. That woman in there is a self-indulgent fool." She tilted her head toward the master bedroom. "The boys are both green and self-absorbed. They're not ready to take over. Sebastian, although we had our differences, could be depended upon to act for the good of the family and the business, even if we didn't always agree on the same means to that end. And that disgraceful girl, Celeste, in some ways she knows more about the business than anyone else now knows or should know. I hope you have interrogated her very closely. And she certainly knows more about men that I ever learned in eight decades of life. She doesn't scare me exactly, but I'm not sure who she's working for anymore. Maybe I never knew."

Nodding, I leaned back in my chair. "Perhaps, Miss Rachel, she'd like to be working for you. That's something to think about if you haven't been involved in day to day operations for more than a dozen years."

"Fourteen, to be exact."

"Then I think you might be able to bring her over

to your side. Maybe she knows too much to be working for someone else in your business. I don't know, but in this situation, that's the first question I would be asking myself. She suggested to me that there's some rivalry among the vineyards in your town that's not altogether healthy."

Miss Rachel freed one hand from the cane to wave this idea away. Perhaps she didn't feel it was worth her consideration. Or it could've been that she'd lived with it so long it no longer concerned her. Age had not softened her; perhaps it never would. I could imagine the boys, Luca and Rocco, simply leaning her body stiffly into a dry, shadowy corner when she died.

I considered whether to tell her that the poker which had once been in the fireplace she sat facing was one of two potential murder weapons that matched the injury on the back of Sebastian's head. Delgado didn't know about her cane because she must've had it with her when she was ejected from the house. Using this context to bring her up to date didn't seem right, nor was I the person to tell her that. I'd wait for Delgado to bring it up in his own time, which would be after one of us in the Agency told him about the cane, because I sensed that was coming.

"So where do we leave this?" I said in a conciliatory tone.

"Go on, then, just go on with it as you have

been." She waved the cane at the cold mouth of the fire-place. "What else can I do here? Find out who killed my nephew. Let us both hope it's not one of the family. I'll give your agency a big bonus if it's someone else."

She rose and offered me her hand, which was not as cold as I expected, but still colder than mine.

"Then I have one more question," I said. "Did your nephew have any visitors the night he fell?"

"I didn't see anyone. But I go to bed at an early hour and it's possible that someone might have arrived after I left this room. You might ask Rathbone, of course, if he let anyone in."

"Can I ask you what time that was?"

"I went to my room at about half past eight and read for a while. I may have turned out the light a little after nine-thirty, although I woke up easily when Rathbone summoned me."

As I walked back down the stairs I couldn't help but think what a disincentive this bonus would be to conclude that it was Miss Rachel herself who had killed Sebastian Cavaletti.

CHAPTER EIGHT
CODY WILLIAMS AND MAYA SANCHEZ

I don't think I should...I know I'm not supposed to be sitting out in the garden. It's my working time and this courtyard is only for the people who rent. We have our own space in that little room off the pantry. Can't we talk there?"

"It's all right, Ximena. Señor Rathbone asked Carmela if we could sit out here. We have permission." Maya gave her an encouraging smile. It had been her idea to get the girl out of the kitchen, out of the comfort zone of her staff quarters, and out of the sense of being under the thumb of the cook nearby.

"But won't they see us? Señor Rathbone doesn't like us talking during work hours." Ximena looked up and back toward the kitchen, which had no windows on the courtyard.

They settled inside a circle of palms and ferns, where a circular cast iron table had been set with a tray holding carafes of coffee and water. No one seemed eager to touch them. To one side a rustic pool offered refuge to half a dozen varieties of pampered exotic fish. Hovering near the surface, one with patches of orange and black watched them calmly with bulging eyes, his fins tracing arabesques through the water.

"You can talk to us here. Can you tell us your full name?" Cody said. They already knew it, but this would establish a pattern of the girl answering their questions.

"I am called Ximena Luz Altamirano." She folded her hands on the edge of the table, her fingers working as if trying to untie a cluster of knots too small to see.

"Thank you. We're trying to find out what happened to Señor Cavaletti," Maya said in an offhand tone, but one that still held a trace of authority. "We want to ask you a few questions about the time that led up to his fall down the stairs. Do you remember where you were that night?" According to staff schedules she should've long since gone home for the day. But Rathbone's manner had suggested to Cody that there was more awaiting them beneath the surface.

A moment of silence followed. "I do not know him, the Señor Cavaletti. I only work in the kitchen and he does not come in there. I do not serve at the table when he eats." She stared down at the figured cast iron surface before her.

Maya studied her for a moment, thinking that the cook, in her chef's clothes, the stained apron, would not be serving the dining table. Did Rathbone serve at dinner? Possibly he would at a formal occasion, but probably not routinely. She made a note to ask Carmela. The impression was growing on her that Ximena had good reason to deny she knew Sebastian.

Ximena was a young woman with fairly light skin, and long hair with enough coarse curl to give it a lot of body. She wore the house staff uniform, a knee-length unbelted blue dress of a durable synthetic fabric, with a white apron that went from her chest to mid thigh, with a certain style, now subdued. Under different and more relaxed circumstances her mobile mouth and lively brown eyes would've made her a standout. But in this stressful moment her apprehensive and clouded manner dampened her appearance. They had not seen her smile a single time. Maya wondered who, if anyone, she had been smiling at before this tragedy. And why was she so frightened?

"We only want to know where you were that night," Cody said gently. "We're trying to place everybody in the house and find out if they might have seen anything."

"But I think Señor Cavaletti must have slipped coming down the stairs. Sometimes he went down very fast because he was in a hurry. Like to meet someone at the door if Señor Rathbone did not answer it."

"Was he expecting someone?"

"I don't know. I don't work so late as that."

Thinking of Rathbone routinely handling the visitors at the entry, Maya tried not to glance at Cody. "But I thought you didn't know him?"

"*Sí*, so I only heard that from the others, the maids who saw him on the steps sometimes, how he was when he walked down so fast. It was like he was running dangerously, you know?" She nodded to underline the truth of her own secondhand observation.

Maya watched Cody's face. It offered nothing, a sure sign that he was thinking something he didn't wish to share. She could not imagine Sebastian, a man in his late fifties, skipping down two flights of unfamiliar steps without a handrail unless he was a dancer. The altitude factor was also part of this mix. Sebastian had lived in Healdsburg, not far from the sea in Northern California, so she guessed it may have been 100 or 200 feet above sea level. San Miguel, at 6400 feet, offered a much thinner kind of air. While visitors often experienced discomfort while hiking up hills and exercising, it was not a problem for those who were used to it.

"Do you have a *novio*?" Maya said. This was a serious boyfriend or a fiancé.

Ximena's hands went up as if keep her at bay. "Oh no, because I am not ready to get married yet. My father is ill and my earnings are needed so much at home."

Cody nodded as if this were the oldest story in the world.

"But is there something happening between you and Carlos, the driver?" Maya said. "Perhaps he might be a good *novio* when you are free to have one later, once your father has recovered. Because like you, Carlos has a steady job with reliable employers."

Ximena's hands nearly ejected the coffee tray in their broad sweep of the table. "That could never be!"

Cody and Maya both waited for a moment in silence for some elaboration of this outburst, since it seemed overdone, but none came.

"But I thought that to me, he seemed like a good young man," Cody finally said. He hadn't met him yet. Ximena shook her head with a suggestion of pride. "Well, that was for a brief time in the past, but he has decided he does not want me now. Poor of him!"

"¡*Qué lástima*!" Maya said. "What a shame! How could Carlos find anyone better than you?"

"I know! This is what I am telling you now." A large tear emerged from each of her eyes. She caught them both in one hand and flung them away toward the fishpond.

Maya noticed a bland look settling over Cody's face. He was on to something.

"I think that boy, Carlos, has unfairly judged you in some way," he said. "Am I right, Señorita Altamirano?"

Biting her lower lip, Ximena shook her head and folded her arms tightly over her breast.

With a look at once informal and sympathetic, Maya leaned forward across the table. "I have noticed that sometimes people don't understand what women do. They can think we mean one thing when we really mean something else. I think this was what happened to you, am I right?" She reached over and pulled Ximena's hand free. The girl did not resist. She nodded as her face crumpled and more tears began to flow. A long moment passed without anyone speaking, although the wheezy sound of the kitchen maid's chest heaving was clear enough.

"This problem was about something that happened between you and Señor Cavaletti, I think? Perhaps you did not expect such a thing from him, an important man like that," Maya added, knowing it was even more likely to come from an important man like that.

Ximena's head twisted away with a pained look.

"How did Carlos find out?" Cody said. With elaborate care, he selected one of the folded linen napkins from the coffee tray, not the top one, and handed it to her. "I don't think anyone from the staff would have said anything about it. They would support you, as we do."

Maya glanced at him in veiled surprise at this level of sensitivity to staff dynamics. She had grown up with three or four staff members in her family house in Mexico City, but she knew most Americans did not have household help.

Ximena covered her face with the napkin. "I told Carlos. I had to tell him because then I had the money for my father's medicine so I didn't need to worry anymore about how I was going to find it for this month. He saw that."

"How much was it?" Cody said softly.

"Señor Cavaletti gave me six hundred pesos for what he made me do," Ximena said from behind the linen fabric. Maya felt she was now veiled like an Arab woman.

"Thirty-one dollars," Cody said unnecessarily to Maya, who had never thought in dollars. The exchange value added nothing to her understanding of what had happened to Ximena. The bottom line was clear enough—it was probably three days pay for her as a kitchen maid.

"But I wouldn't let him be inside me. I could never do that. Can you see that?"

Maya took her other hand, and drawing both of them together palm to palm, held them pressed between hers for the longest time.

CHAPTER NINE

That far into the case I sensed that Rathbone was warming toward us. Our presence over the past three days had been insistent, and most investigations don't require much formality. Quite the opposite, since we like to apply a bit of pressure. So often this business is about getting in people's faces to cause them enough stress to make them act erratically. It doesn't make us many friends, but when people crack under our scrutiny, it can sometimes release a lot of information. It might be only what they want us to believe, but that in itself can be enlightening. At other times they simply try to kill us. That also carries a clear message.

After they filled me in, I realized that Cody and Maya's talk with Ximena had brought about a limited version of this effect, although we were all sympathetic to the way Sebastian had abused her. Why wasn't Celeste enough for him? I had seen more richness and complexity in her than in many women I had known, and in many men as well. Was the appeal of a kitchen maid simply novelty? A naked body he had never seen before? One he could coerce and dominate through his status and his wealth? Ximena was an attractive girl, but why didn't she pale next to the rich and spicy complexity of Celeste? Was coercion itself a value for him in this? I had already repeatedly established in some detail that I didn't know everything about women, but this was making me wonder what I didn't know about men.

Meanwhile, I also considered what Delgado might be up to in the background. Our methods were different enough that we rarely encountered his crew in the field. That was useful when we were both still privately gathering information, but not so much when we asked ourselves, as now, how much the other side knew.

Maybe it was time to tell Delgado about Miss Rachel's cane, but we were still conflicted about doing that, since she was employing us. When or if the moment came that we thought she was a real suspect, that position could change.

In the meantime Miss Rachel had told Rathbone to give the Agency whatever help it needed. When I showed up the following morning unannounced at a quarter before nine o'clock, his eyebrows briefly struggled to avoid expressing his surprise as he opened the door.

"I know it's not the actual crime scene," I said. "But none of us has looked at Mr. Cavaletti's bedroom.

It's one of those lesser details, as you can imagine, that we're now catching up with. Since he didn't plan to die on those stairs, whatever the cause, I still would like to look at his room. It might say something about what he was doing, or thinking, in his last moments. In turn, that might lead us to a real suspect."

After this carefully phrased query did I see an oddly ironic look on Rathbone's face as he twisted a key off his ring and handed it to me? I was getting a cue of some sort from him but I couldn't read it. "Naturally," I continued, "we have already talked to Elizabeth in the master suite."

This drew no comment from him other than a curt nod. "When you leave the main block of the house, turning right as you come out of the bar off the great room, the first long passage will lead you to another right turn, and along that wall facing the courtyard and the main house opposite, the middle bedroom suite of three was that of Mr. Cavaletti."

"Thank you, Rathbone."

"No problem, sir."

But I had not asked why the head of the family had been exiled to the guest wing. Was it by his own choice to allow him some privacy? Anyway, such a question would exceed the limits of Rathbone's discreet opinions.

No one was in sight as I followed the second floor

gallery around and above the courtyard to the middle bedroom. A broad set of four tall casement windows flanked the door on one side. The drapes within were all drawn. On the other side were two higher windows that must have served the bathroom and dressing area. The door was old varnished wood with a linked cluster of carved arabesques below the center rail. I saw no reason to knock.

The key worked easily. With a staff of seven, all the locks in that house must've been as well maintained as everything else. No lamps were lit inside, but the room was dimly illuminated from the borrowed light of the two high windows in the adjacent dressing room complex. I paused to let my eyes adjust to the dimmer light. Outside, the morning was brilliant.

"Don't you ever knock, Paul?" This came from the bed in a husky tone as I heard the door latch softly behind me. It was a woman's voice and the choices of which one it might be were limited.

I peered at the king sized bed against the back wall. There I could pick out the golden highlights in Celeste's hair and her bare arms and shoulders above the sheet. In the vague light the carved headboard behind her displayed a series of saints in contorted positions. Although I couldn't see exactly what they were doing, their moves looked faintly suggestive. Maybe the theme of the piece was the temptation of the Seven Deadly Sins.

Meanwhile some response was required from me.

"I'm really sorry to bother you, Celeste. I didn't think anyone was sleeping in here. Rathbone didn't tell me. Do you want me to go away, since you're obviously not up yet? I can come back later."

She ignored the last part. "Maybe he didn't know I was in here," she said. "Or maybe he's too discreet to be curious about what other people are up to in this house. That would be a good fit for his role in the Cavaletti family."

Or maybe he knows every bloody detail of what goes on here and he wanted to set up this encounter, I thought. Was he a fantasy matchmaker of some kind with a twisted sense of humor? For him the frustrations of working for the Cavalettis must've run both broad and deep.

"Come over here and sit by me, Paul." Her voice took on a tone at once more hospitable and alert. She placed a palm on the embroidered coverlet not far from her side.

I sat next to her on the designated spot. From that point I could see her much better.

"Just to start, I want you to know that I'm naked under here." She said this with an angelic smile, using two fingers to lift the top edge of the sheet an inch and let it fall again.

I gave her an appreciative smile. "That's good.

I guess all of us are naked under something." I lifted the hem of my shirt with two fingers and released it. It didn't have quite the same effect. "Does being naked make you more frank? I know it always does with me. You wouldn't believe how blunt with other people I can be in the shower. Of course there's rarely anyone there to appreciate it."

She shook her head. "No. Nothing ever makes me more frank. I'm already at full frankness all the time." She pulled one of the broad pillows behind her neck to brace her head and shoulders at a better angle.

"Full frontal frankness," I suggested.

She nodded immediately. "That's the way I think of it too."

"And that's exactly what I want from you, since we've been accidentally reconnected like this. Let's start with Sebastian. We talked before about Elizabeth, a little about the boys, and more about Miss Rachel. But you said little about your boss. I came here to get more information on what he was about. What did he want? I came this morning to search this room, but you'll be a better resource, I'm sure."

"Then turn on the lamp and I'll tell you. I want to see you better. You're kind of backlit from those high windows. You know, in this light I think your hair might be thinning a little on top. I'm catching a trace of glare off your scalp."

Trying to take this as a compliment, I reached over and switched it on. With more light, and without any makeup, Celeste looked as good as she had during our talk on the terrace. A glow of warmth came off her body through the bed linens and a subtly intimate scent rose from her skin. Around her neck was a fine silver chain with an unusual link design. I couldn't see what the pendant might have been, but from the way it was hanging it was carrying some weight below the edge of the sheet.

"Why was Sebastian here? Was it for more than the food and wine festival? Because that wouldn't require a month's stay; that show only lasts four days."

"Sebastian was also looking at property. I'm sure you know there are a number of vineyards here. A family named Mendoza has fourteen hundred acres on a dirt road off the highway to Querétaro, just before you get to the Jalpa turnoff. Sebastian looked at it two days before he died and he liked it very much. The drainage, the character of the soil, the orientation of the slopes, and some of the other factors he wanted were all favorable. He brought away a dozen soil samples for testing when we get home. The rainfall distribution was not quite what he needed, but the land has water rights and the vines could be irrigated to make it work. Best of all, the Mendozas were willing to sell a portion of it, since fourteen hundred acres was far more than Cavaletti Vineyards required. Sebastian was thinking more like eighty or a hundred that had the right characteristics."

I looked at her for a moment. "But how handy would it be to set up and manage that? We're so distant from Northern California here."

She nodded slowly. "That's right, but for a long time he'd wanted to experiment with some varieties of grapes that don't do so well in Healdsburg. This area is much better suited to them. He was thinking of using a name like Pedregal Estate, or something that reflected a different location, one of merit, but still under the Cavaletti Vineyards umbrella. They'd all be estate bottled and show the vintage year, of course."

"Did Miss Rachel support this idea?"

"Not at all. It made her spit the few times we talked about it at dinner. She doesn't tell me much about anything, but I think she came along to head off a purchase, in case Sebastian got too close. He would've needed her signature if he had to borrow money to do the deal. And he told me that Elizabeth didn't like the idea, either. Both of those women hate to travel."

"Even in the household jet."

"Yes. My observation is that the more privileged you are the harder you are to please. Elizabeth whines the whole time after take off, and Miss Rachel is a white-knuckle flier. She keeps both hands locked on her cane in front of her and her expression makes her look like her dentures don't fit as well in higher altitudes. I always have to wait on everybody when we travel and Elizabeth went through about half a bottle of Grey Goose on the rocks during the flight coming down. She had to be taken off on a gurney, but they had phoned ahead for that before we left San Francisco. They knew it would happen."

"I'm sure Rathbone made that call."

"Exactly. You're a quick study, by the way."

"So if he bought this property near Jalpa, Sebastian would have to travel down here alone to get that vineyard started."

Her bare shoulders shrugged as they tested the edge of the sheet. "Not entirely alone, Paul, but surely without them. I like to think of it as alone in important ways that would generate less interference and more opportunity. Naturally Sebastian would need someone to handle his email traffic. I told you how he was about computers." She regarded me calmly with her luminous brown eyes. "He'd also need someone to take the kinks out of his muscles at the end of the day. A person who could care for him in ways that Rathbone couldn't."

I wondered whether some of his muscles might be kinkier than the others. "A person franker than Rathbone. One who could be more direct with those rigid tissues."

"Yes, exactly, and meanwhile Rathbone could stay home in Sonoma County and answer the door."

"Of course. I can see it perfectly."

"He's *very* effective at that." Her tone seemed to suggest that there were certainly other things that some of us were very good at too.

Throughout this exchange Celeste had still been subtly working her spell on me and I now had the sudden idea of taking her by the shoulders and pulling her against my chest. My fingers were itching to probe her naked back for any tension, to examine the alignment of her vertebrae, but that would've gone somewhat beyond my most polished interviewing style, one I had worked on in numerous cases in the past. Besides, my hand still ached from the last time I touched her. You never forget a touch like that.

It was time to explore a new angle to this investigation, and Maya had briefed me about the conversation with Ximena, so in the same spirit of frankness that Celeste so strongly favored, I decided to bring it up.

"How did Sebastian get along with the household staff here?"

"When he noticed them, I guess he got along with some better than others. I know he didn't care much for Carlos, the driver. Sebastian demanded a certain amount of deference from the people around him, and when he didn't get it, he quickly moved on. That was why he asked me to set up a car service for him earlier, on the day before he died."

"Did he have an opportunity to use it?"

"He never did."

"Was there some other reason for his problem with Carlos, or was it only bad chemistry? Sometimes you can get off on the wrong foot with people, especially if it's in a country you're not familiar with. It takes a while to grasp the nuance of foreign manners and customs."

Celeste looked at me for a long moment. Her lips were slightly parted and I glimpsed her tongue at the edges of her teeth. "So you already know about Sebastian and Ximena, don't you? I guess that's what you do. Excuse me for selling you short."

"That's what I *try* to do, Celeste. It doesn't always work. Not everyone I talk to is as frank as you are. It's kind of refreshing for me not to have to pussyfoot around a case all the time. How did you find out about it?"

She looked away. "Six days ago I saw them outside this room where we are now. I was about to come out here from the main house but I stopped at the edge of the door. Sebastian was holding that kitchen girl by the shoulders and she had her hands on him too, with her palms pressing against his chest, like she was pushing him away. I knew then what was coming."

"Are you suggesting Sebastian had a problem with women?"

"No, it was never a problem for him. He always went after most of the good-looking women he met.

Some didn't go for it, but others did. He was a mature and attractive man with considerable power and a lot of money. Don't think I didn't understand that, since it's a winning combination anywhere, not just here in the kitchen. Ximena was kind of a low point for him. Maybe that was just an off day." At the end of this sentence her tone had gotten bitter, but still, as if she understood this better than anyone, she shrugged more affirmatively, which nearly displaced the coverlet to a dangerous level. In this business I was used to mixed messages, but this one brought some new elements to the blend.

For a moment I thought about her statement that Sebastian hadn't hit it off with Carlos. How far had that been reciprocated on the driver's part? I set it aside for later as not a question that Celeste could answer.

"Why did Sebastian marry Elizabeth? Did he ever tell you? Maybe you didn't ask."

"I asked him that same thing one afternoon at home when he'd been complaining about her. What he told me was that she was the daughter of a prizewinning winemaker that his father was determined to keep on at the vineyard in that critical transition to premium wines. It was a business relationship on Sebastian's end, you might say, to accommodate his father. Naturally, Elizabeth was wild about him."

"That seems to be the ongoing trend around here." I studied her reaction to this and found none. "I was told he had movie star good looks."

"Even now, but more like the smooth major hunk type of character than the wild kid on a Harley."

"So what was your position?"

"I was the one he came home to. I was the one on salary, the one who could also send in his payroll, juggle the books when necessary, keep his wife at arm's length, and rub him the right way. That was my role. I always knew what he liked best, and I cared enough to get it right. That counts for a lot with anyone." She regarded me coolly for a while, as if waiting when I made no response to this. Celeste appeared to have a detailed kind of canniness that enabled her to adapt well, but still fell short of wisdom. She clearly understood the nuance of her experience. "You don't seem to be judging me much," she finished.

I shook my head and smiled. "I only ask the questions. Judgment isn't my job, nor is it my inclination. It's people's connections that always interest me. I mainly want to know who was here at the house and where they were. So on that night he fell, where were you? The coroner said he died between eleven o'clock and midnight."

She patted the mattress with her palm. "I was right here, in this same bed, naked and waiting."

"I see." Thinking no one could confirm this.

"Just like I am now, Paul." Her steady look was not obviously provocative, but neither was it innocent.

The best word for it I could think of was *frank*.

"Did he leave you to see someone?"

"No, I hadn't seen him since we finished dinner at a little after eight o'clock."

I won't try to describe her look through the last part of this exchange, but somehow I was able to exit Sebastian's bedroom with no further injuries. Celeste could wait a while longer for another conversation. I suspected she had more detail available if I could find the right questions. Even though I had nothing to explain, I looked narrowly around the courtyard before I slipped out the door. Celeste's commitment to frankness was certainly impressive, although at times it could be a little too personal for my comfort, and she knew that. In all of the Paul Zacher Agency's sixteen past cases I've never gotten involved with a suspect and I had no intention of breaking that record. As for her plans, I couldn't quite read them, but I knew she was shopping for a new employer, and she appeared to be offering a rather compelling internship as a way to demonstrate her skills. Not that I could ever be so easily distracted from the main tasks of a case.

As I skirted the courtyard back to the main house I realized I had lost track of my original intent and forgotten to take a close look at any of Sebastian Cavaletti's personal possessions.

Well, maybe just one.

CHAPTER TEN

I feel like someone is missing from this picture," I said to Cody on my cell as I was driving home that morning. The image of Celeste's face against the pillow was still in my mind. "Shouldn't we also look at the pilot of the family jet? Did anything happen on the plane coming down? Given how contorted this is getting, I wouldn't be surprised if he had his own story to add to the mix. But he didn't appear on the list of residents we got from Rathbone. He must not be at the house. "

I had already given Cody a slightly sanitized version of my latest encounter with Celeste. I didn't get into her wardrobe issues, since not every detail needs to appear in our casebook summary at the end. Just because some information might be interesting doesn't mean it's also relevant. The skillful investigator can always distinguish between the two.

I heard him shifting around on the other end of the line as if his chair might be scraping on a tile floor. Cody lived on the third floor level of a condo building on Prologación Aldama where his shallow balcony over-looked a small manicured courtyard garden far below. He liked to take his morning coffee there as he read the news off the Internet on his laptop.

"Don't worry about that, Paul. I got his name from Rathbone and I already checked him out. That guy is a commercial jet pilot based in San Francisco, former Air Force with a combat record in Iraq and Afghanistan. The way it works is that he flies you in, he arranges to fly you back out when you're done, but on a longer stay like this he doesn't wait for you. If your plane isn't working full time, he still is. He's flying a lot of other people around in their personal or company jets. It's part of a network of private pilots with a steady stream of assign-ments that fit the planes each one is licensed to fly, and that's usually just a few. When he brought the Cavalettis in at León he turned around and was gone on the next commercial flight back to the U.S. The stamp on his passport wasn't even dry. He never got any further into México than the airport."

"And that was how long before Sebastian died?"

"Eight days."

"Is he the same pilot they always use?"

"Rathbone says they try to, although it's not pos-sible every time because of scheduling. But it mostly works that way if they can book it far enough ahead. After using him for five years, the Cavalettis are very comfortable with him."

"Might he know something from all that coming and going with them?"

"Absolutely. I've got a note to talk to him when he comes back to fly them out, if he's the one to do it."

"Did Rathbone say where else Sebastian liked to go?"

"Yes, he did, and he said it with what was nearly a wink, which surprised the hell out of me. Maybe since Sebastian's gone now he feels he can loosen up a bit."

"And the answer is?"

"For his own vacations he preferred Rio."

"Wow! He must've been a quite the player! But that's all up in the air now." Indeed it was, with Sebastian and his plane both grounded. I said goodbye to Cody.

I had gone about a kilometer farther when I realized that we might have been unconsciously avoiding the two boys, Luca and Rocco. I recalled that Luca was thirty and Rocco was twenty-seven. This made Luca the heir apparent, although they each owned ten percent of the business. That kind of minority share did not give them a motive, only a slice of the profits that they must have already had for some time.

Celeste had been dismissive of both of them, which for me now raised a red flag. I'd come across frankness before in this business and it did not always mean honesty. It could simply be a style that underlined what people wanted us to think. Realizing I should have done it earlier, I pulled over to fill my tank and dialed Rathbone. Of course he was polite, although he may have sighed when he saw my number come up again on his screen.

"How about Luca? I'd like to talk to him." I said when he answered. It was almost a relief that I didn't have to be as indirect as I did here every day with Mexicans. With Americans and their butlers you could put it right between their eyes, like they did to us when they came down here.

"I'm afraid he is out playing tennis at the moment, sir."

"Why be afraid? Is he playing one of the Williams sisters? Then when is he expected back, if his knees can survive that encounter?"

"When he has played enough, sir. As always, Mr. Luc will be the judge of that."

"Impeccable logic, Rathbone, but could you speculate on a time? I really do need to talk to him. Or do you wish to give me his cell number? I have to verify the spelling on the engraving for his trophy."

"Unfortunately, that is prohibited by household policy, sir."

No higher authority, certainly, than that. "Then please bear a message to him from me. I would like to meet with him today at four this afternoon. Let me know his response, if you will. He can choose the place."

Clearly the death of his father had not slowed Luca's sporting life. In fact, few of the family members and their entourage that I had met were exactly prostrate with grief. I'd had a tearless and quite businesslike phone conversation with Miss Rachel right after my second meeting with her where she told me that Sebastian's remains had been released by the coroner and would shortly be cremated. They would be returning to California on the family jet when the party went home, if it ever did (her phrasing). A memorial was being planned for Healdsburg at an as yet undetermined date. Most of this seemed to irritate more than move her. This reminded me that older folks often don't like change. Maybe she was more offended by Sebastian's death than saddened by it. In the normal sequence of things, his passing had been out of order.

Life goes on, I thought, in a more conciliatory tone than anyone else was using. Possibly the heart of this case might lie in the connections that were now quietly reforming in the background. It was like a reshuffling of dancers after one partner has unexpectedly left the floor, a moment of confusion before they began to move together again in different combinations. Would Ximena and Carlos get back together? Would he forgive her and she forgive him for not forgiving her earlier? In redefining her position, who else was Celeste trolling for besides me? The available waters were extensive. How would Miss Rachel and Rathbone get along in Sebastian's absence? What did the future hold for the two boys, Luca and Rocco, whose personal views on life and family I felt I now needed to hack into?

Maybe Sebastian had been swept from the board like a carelessly placed pawn in a larger game, although that seemed to underestimate his importance. I was thinking about this as I pulled into a lucky parking place five doors down from mine on Quebrada when my phone went off.

"Mr. Paul Zacher, please."

"Hello Rathbone. Did you connect?"

"Yes, sir. Mr. Luc would like to meet you at three o'clock this afternoon at the rooftop bar of the Overlook Palace Hotel if that is convenient in all respects."

"I'll be there. Thank you, Rathbone."

"No problem, sir. Enjoy your meeting."

A bit early for cocktail hour perhaps, but with these wine people drinking anytime had to be a way of life.

The Overlook Palace is a newer hotel in the colonial style close in between the Parque Juarez and the Ancha de San Antonio, a wide street traveling south out of downtown. It is three tall stories high and the bar on the roof offers views that encourage guests to settle in and relax with a sense of both perspective and scale not so easily available in most of our small, narrow sixteenth and seventeenth century streets below. The clientele tends to be upscale, often from Los Angeles, Mexico City or nearby Querétaro, and the service is attentive even as the waiters try to avoid getting between the guests and the vistas.

At three o'clock that day, in the determined glare of a July afternoon, only four people were sitting in the bar area. One young couple in broad-brimmed straw hats held hands and faced the view toward the Parroquia, our grand "parish church" on the plaza downtown, the *jardín*. Another, a woman of about fifty in designer sunglasses and a visor that left her curly hair exposed, nursed a glass of white wine as she shuffled through her cell phone apps with the tip of her index finger. The single man who rose and placed his palms together at my approach had to be Luca Cavaletti.

Even so, I hesitated slightly because he had dense blond hair, which Italians don't commonly have, although they're fine with the dense part. On the other hand, I knew that many blondes and redheads can be found in the north of Italy, descended from the Lombards. In any case, he appeared to be expecting me. He was wearing white linen shorts, which local adults don't do here, but then, he was playing by California rules. He also wore an expensive monogrammed sport shirt with a light sweater draped over his shoulders. Its arms were looped about his neck. As we shook hands I could see how very bright his teeth were, even though he wasn't facing the sun and I was.

"Paul Zacher! How are you? Nice to meet you. Please call me Luc."

"Of course."

"Have a seat." He gestured to a cushioned settee fronting a teak coffee table. On it were two stemmed glasses and an open bottle of red wine. The cork lay nearby waiting to be sniffed like a girl with an orchid in her hair. A waiter hastened over to open a broad umbrella over us. This told me Luc had just walked in long enough before to order and open the bottle.

Luc's face took on a serious expression. "This is the '04 Cavaletti Gran Reserva. I took the liberty of having it opened to breathe a bit. I wanted to meet you here because the Overlook does such a great job with Cavaletti wines. Naturally they fell all over me when I came in and passed out my card to the staff." He grinned modestly.

"I hope you weren't badly injured. Mexicans can be so demonstrative in their heartfelt joy."

If you are going to come on being so full of yourself, then make the contents more substantial. Taking this without irony, Luc waved my concerns aside. "It's all business anyway, isn't it?"

"It certainly is for me." There are times when I'd rather be painting. This was starting to look like one of them. "I wanted to tell you how sorry I was to hear of your father's passing. I didn't know him, but any time it's so unexpected it has to be that much more difficult for the family."

"Well, yes, and thank you for that. In so many ways my dad was still in his prime."

I made a note to ask Celeste whether she'd noticed his powers waning. Luc's face did not express much grief. Perhaps a family like the Cavalettis had a brave public façade to maintain and did their mourning in private.

"He was down here to negotiate the acquisition of a new vineyard property," Luc went on. "The food and wine fiesta was only a cover for that, since he didn't wish any word of what he was doing to leak out back home."

"I did hear that. Would it have been damaging to your family's interests to have that become known?"

Before answering this, Luc decanted a dollop of the '04 into his own deep glass, inhaled it, sipped it, rolled it around in his mouth, chewed it subtly, audibly swallowed it with an expression of delight, and then poured my glass a quarter full before he refilled his own. "I don't know that it would've been a problem, but no one at home likes anyone else to get the jump on them when they're planning something new. That secrecy is no more than a reflex, a deeply-rooted habit among old rivals."

"Does it have anything to do with the Cavaletti origins as a maker of jug wines?"

"Ah! I can see Miss Rachel has already given you something of our business history. The truth is that everything we do now is aimed at reinforcing that image of being the super premium winemakers. It's practically automatic. *Jug* is not a word that ever comes up in our conversations. At home, I mean. I hope nobody heard me say that now."

"I can see that, but will your mother be able to continue that tradition, given her condition?" As he considered this, I tasted the wine. I could find no other word than delightful. It was rich, round, full of character and nuance, and while I'm no connoisseur, it was far, far better than the Chilean red Maya and I drank at home. It was a bottle worthy of a special occasion. More than only trying to make an impression, I began to feel that Luc was being generous to me, but perhaps that was an impression he wished to make too. I had heard this was an industry that operated on wide margins, and the private jet and the rental of a prestigious San Miguel mansion testified to that.

"I guess you've already met my mother." His voice dropped as if someone might overhear. I didn't contradict him, although so far it had been only Maya who had talked to her. At that moment, from somewhere lost in the stucco labyrinth of the old city below, a siren wail clawed upward toward us as it wound through the narrow streets. In Luc's company, I had felt like we were above problems of that kind. Of course, there was the murder of Sebastian five days before. The desperate sound from below brought that home to me again.

At around six feet, my height, Luc had features that were clear and almost sculpted, with an elegantly shaped nose. His lips were firm and they formed a good line. I could've taken up a pencil and sketched his face in a heartbeat. Had he displayed more character rather than just fine modeling in his appearance, he could almost have been a candidate for one of my more insightful portraits. But as I studied him I could find no pain there, no disappointment, and little self-doubt. His skin was a smooth landscape with no visible scars. While his look was all about where he was going, it offered few hints of where he had been. Of course, he was only thirty. Come back in ten years and we'll talk about doing a painting, I thought. Show me then the damage to your heart and the strains to your character as they appear in your face. The impact of his father's death had not emerged there yet. I wondered how long it would take.

"You're enjoying this wine, aren't you," he said. It was not a question. With a serenely professional expression he held his glass up against the angular light. In that position I could see that the blocky letters on his massive gold class ring spelled Stanford.

"Very much. Thank you for opening it for this meeting."

He nodded. "Not a problem. Personally I would rank this bottle as number seven in what we have on sale right now. My father thought of it as number six. That was one of our very minor disagreements."

"So insignificant, I'm sure, and probably more a matter of personal taste than any absolute difference in standards between you. Were there other issues, though, more serious?" Here was a concern— was the current generation of connoisseurs challenging the previous one? Do individual palates, no matter how experienced, become outmoded? After all, Luc's was the *successor* generation, one of several in a line, at Cavaletti Vineyards.

Luc shrugged. "Nothing to speak of. Our goals were identical, and all of our best product is bottled under the Cavaletti name, although we own six other labels." It was not a Mexican shrug, which can carry the burden of all of life's uncertainties focused on the head of a pin. His was more a lightweight shrug. It said *Nothing at this level matters*, rather than México's *Everything matters, but sorting it out is beyond us, so we all simply go on*. Sometimes believing in fate can be more comforting than trying to explain complex events. Luc poured us a second round, which opened another level to the conversation as well. I took it up.

"And then there's Celeste," I said. "Perhaps she's a catalyst of sorts in this story." As Luc set the bottle back on the table his hand did not tremble, although his eyes took on a distant look.

"Yes, and now some of the second glass subjects will rise to the surface of this conversation." Luc's expression said he thought he was ready for that, but I wondered if he was. He looked like he could handle anything that fell within the bounds of normalcy. Beyond that range, perhaps not as much. I could see that Luc thought he was cool, but for me, being cool can only begin when you're out of your comfort zone.

"Who is she?" I said quietly.

"I can tell you her last name, which will mean nothing at all in answer to that question." He paused there. If he'd had a moustache he would've been twisting it.

"And I already know it. I can tell you in the same spirit of revelation," I said, "that I found her extremely attractive. Not only in her appearance, but I liked her frankness. There is something uniquely fearless about her in what she says and how she says it. I think she would go up against anyone. That makes me curious about how she related to your father. I'm sure he must have been quite formidable himself."

He looked at me for a moment. "I believe you also think she's dangerous."

"Yes, I do, especially at close quarters."

Luc held his glass in both hands as if to warm it, then took a long pull of the wine. He glanced at me as if to assess how much more I knew, but I had played a lot of poker in college and I can still do the face quite well.

"This is so strange," he said, "because I don't know you, and I've never talked in detail about Celeste and my father to anyone before. Some other people have observed their connection, of course, over the past three years. I'm sure they must have speculated about how far it went."

"I don't have to remind you that your father is gone now, so perhaps this is the right time to have this conversation. There is some question as to how he died, and any information you can give me might contribute to answering it."

He nodded slowly. "My father knew a lot of women, OK? His primary attachment was never to my mother. Once I got old enough to understand about such things, I always thought of it as a dynastic marriage. They're usually about business or politics. But for Celeste (here Luc's hand gesture became wavy and imprecise for an instant) Dad had developed a special connection. I say that now, and I hear how common it must sound to you, but that's still a way to put it that's too superficial. I want to make the point that it was *deep*."

This started the computer part of my mind shuffling and whirring through all the old worn punch cards of desire. It finished with the essential body warmth that exuded from Celeste's skin while I spoke with her on the bed, the feathery caress of her breath on my face. I realized now that this was only a tiny part of her range. "Was that something he told you?"

Luc chuckled ironically. "Dad never said anything to me about her, not a single word from the time she came to us. It was like there she was one day and no explanations were necessary. I only observed what I know from interacting with the two of them over business matters. And often at dinner, of course."

"What did they like to talk about?"

"The vineyard operations, mostly. He also enjoyed discussing winemaking as an art. She was a good listener, and she gave you the sense of making the most of her connections to advance herself. I don't know that much about her background, but I think she came from humble beginnings. And they both loved theater. That was a popular subject with them."

"Did that close relationship prevent him from chasing other women?" I already knew it hadn't, but this was more about discovering what Luc knew.

"Not at all. Commitment was a virtue Dad could

understand, but exclusivity was never on his radar. For him the two did not intersect."

I nodded slowly. That would often not have been a contradiction in México either.

"Were you at home on the night he died? I'm wondering if he had any guests. I asked Rathbone that and I thought his answer was equivocal, saying he hadn't been on duty at the door for the entire time. He seemed to be protecting the family in his own mind, or even himself, but he might have been inadvertently protecting the killer. Not something he would do intentionally, of course."

"Have you determined that it was a murder?"

"The evidence I've seen supports that."

"I went out right after nine-thirty that night."

"Where did you go?"

"I went to the Boardwalk for the first time."

The Boardwalk is a nightclub downtown on Calle Reloj with music and an active social scene. I noted the fact that Luc found it necessary to tell me that was the first time he had gone. From Rathbone I knew that he was married with a five-year-old daughter.

"When I got home at close to one o'clock the police were already there and they wouldn't let me in the house. Miss Rachel was leaving with Rocco and Celeste. One of the cops had my mother in a wheelchair. They were all bitching about the way they were being treated on an occasion like that, a family tragedy. I left with them. I was a little drunk and like everybody else, I was completely stunned."

"Had the driver taken you downtown earlier?"

"Yes, that was Carlos, but I took a cab back. He understood that I would."

"What about the staff on your return?"

"Rathbone had collected Carmela and Luis on the other end of the parking area. A uniformed officer was watching them. I don't know where they stayed that night, but Rathbone arranged something for them. The other staff people had gone home long before that. The family all came here to the Overlook Palace. Carlos was already gone so Rathbone drove us in the Suburban. We were lucky to find a place with enough rooms on no notice, but it was a slow part of the week."

"Did your father see anyone that night?"

"Not as far as I knew. The last I saw of him was at dinner around seven forty-five or eight. I never saw him again."

"Was your mother at that dinner?"

"No. She always eats in her room, even at home. It's much easier for her because then she doesn't have to dress. I haven't seen her dressed in years."

"How about Celeste?"

"She was at the table."

"Does she usually eat with you at home, too?"

"She does if she's there working. Celeste is like family. She and my dad often worked irregular hours." He said this without irony. "And Rocco?"

"Yes, he was there. You'll probably want to interview him."

"Any special reason I should?"

"You'll discover that when you talk to him. He has a different take on things, you know? He likes to go his own way." Luc divided the last of the wine between our glasses. As he gazed out over the city his lips were compressed into a thin line.

"Is he active in the business?"

An ironic smile came across his face. "I would have to say that he's more active in avoiding the business."

Luc's equivocal introduction of his brother only further piqued my interest in talking to him. "Any idea who might've wanted to kill your father?"

Luc looked at me over the rim of his glass. "I don't envy you your job."

"Why is that?"

"I can see a number of people with motives."

"For example."

"I don't want to tell tales out of school."

"Class is over. Let's start with the obvious."

"Well, my mother. She's spent most of her married life sidelined, even though her husband was the head of one of Sonoma County's most prestigious wine families. She should've been socially prominent. She should've spent her time on the board of charities and cutting ribbons for new facilities."

"But isn't she hiding in a blind of her own making?"

"Yes, but that doesn't make her any less angry. This way she gets to blame Dad and Celeste for what she's done to herself, as well as what they did to her. She's doubled down her cards. In her mind it'll be twice the revenge, twice the fun. Maybe Dad's death was only the beginning. Maybe Celeste should be watching her back now."

"OK, but didn't your mother also disable her ability to take action against them?"

"So it seems."

"So it seems?"

"Yes. Maybe it only looks that way. I honestly don't know what she's capable of in terms of getting around. It was four or five years ago when I last saw her on her own feet without leaning on someone else."

"Can the personal assistant tell us anything?"

"I doubt it. This one is only a temp furnished by the house manager. Elena is not even full time. She helps Mom get going in the morning, stays with her for a while, and comes back in the evening to get her settled in bed. The one at home is the person you need to talk to."

Privately I wondered how forthcoming that person might be if we spoke to her. We had encountered them once or twice on other cases, and personal assistants tended to be just that, and dedicated to their employer.

"And then? How about Miss Rachel?"

"Truly a character out of Dickens, I think, or Nathaniel Hawthorne. Someone from *The House of the Seven Gables*. Once intelligent and able, but now twisted with age, jealousy and anger. She no longer sees the world around her with clarity or objectivity. She would prefer to remake it, if she could. Failing that, she's determined to ignore it."

"Could she have killed him?"

"How exactly did my father die?"

"A blow to the back of his head sent him spinning head over heels down those stairs. Multiple skull fractures and the brain swelling they brought on killed him." Luc nodded slowly. "Poor Dad. A blow to the back of the head. Have you ever taken a look at her cane?"

CHAPTER ELEVEN

Of course in the Agency we're always happy when a conversation, like the one with Luc, underlined an abrasive issue. It's a sign that you can't ignore it anymore. All three of us had been wrestling with the same problem, although none of us had brought it up yet. We had an ongoing ethical issue with Miss Rachel's cane to deal with.

What must have happened was clear enough. Upon the discovery of Sebastian's body by Rathbone, Miss Rachel had been awakened and called the police. Delgado responded with his crew and they ushered the family and staff outside while they secured the house. Miss Rachel certainly would've been walking with her cane around the steps at the front door, even though she had taken the elevator down, and before the eyes of the police, strolled outside with one of the two potential murder weapons in her hand, the other being the great room fireplace poker.

Even without this prod from Luc, Cody had

reached Maya at home while I was still talking to him at the mansion. It was time, Cody told her, for a sit down to sort out our options. She had suggested we didn't have many, and I already knew that. When I arrived home I started a batch of guacamole and Maya ran to the store for some chips, *totopos*. When Cody arrived at five we were ready. I wasn't fond of the idea that I was going to switch to the Chilean red after Luc's Gran Reserva, but as Maya had said, we didn't have many options. When we adjourned to the loggia in back, at the edge of our garden, I poured a round.

"Well," Cody began, "I think it's time we dealt with the cane issue because it puts us increasingly in a bad light. Although it's not as clear here in México as it was years ago in Illinois, in my mind we're all officers of the court, and that means we have some obligations to local law enforcement. And, I will suggest too, haven't we always acted that way in the past? Even if we never spelled it out, that's always been our policy."

"That's going to put Miss Rachel in a tough spot," Maya said, with a discontented twist to her lips. "Maybe she can handle it or maybe she's too old to be as tough as she thinks she is."

"We can't predict what Delgado will think or do if we give him that information," I said.

"We've turned in clients before," Cody said. "Subtly, of course. But this is not a matter of turning her in, because from the evidence so far and the absence of a motive, I don't think that Miss Rachel killed Sebastian. But even so, we know about the cane and Delgado doesn't. That's the bottom line. I don't like to sound high-minded, but we're supposed to be serving the needs of justice, and without telling Delgado about this key bit of evidence, we're not. As it is now, we're withholding evidence."

"I'm not comfortable with this either way," I said. "I knew this conversation was coming but that didn't help me get ready for it. We had this same kind of problem in Oaxaca with that case we filed as *Strike Zone*, when we had all that Aztec gold and we had to decide who owned it."

"We've always had to be our own ethics committee," Maya added, without much enthusiasm.

Cody reached into his shirt pocket and pulled out a letter size sheet that had been folded into quarters. It was a copy of our intake form for the case. Maya had printed one for each of us. He pointed to the bottom of the page, specifically to the block that was headed: The *Client's Objective*. There I had crossed out the words *Prove Nephew's Death an Accident*, and substituted the words, *Solve the Case as a Murder*.

"As it turns out, we were originally hired to do a cover up," Cody said, "and the person who hired us may well become the chief suspect once we tell Delgado about that cane."

"And this paper would only reinforce that outcome," I said. Of course, we regarded all of our own
internal documents of a case as confidential and we
would never have turned any of them over to the police.

There are times in this business when you make
some stupid mistake and a criminal escapes, or someone is killed and you think you might have prevented it
if you had approached things differently. What we had
before us now was another kind of dilemma, where you
might harm your client by doing the correct and honorable thing. To some degree this was relative, since I also
didn't believe that Miss Rachel had killed her nephew.
But what Delgado might think in this situation was more
important than what any of us thought, and not for the
first time.

"I think we have to tell Delgado," Maya said. "I
can't see any other way. Any other thoughts?"

None of us had a single one.

As head of the Paul Zacher Agency, a role she
took quite seriously, Maya accepted the challenge and
went downtown to talk to Delgado the next morning. He
tended to treat her with more deference than he gave
Cody and me, and it seemed right that she should have
to take this on, since she had also used her position now
and then to dodge the occasional nasty task and pass it

on to us. On our last case, one we filed as *The Jericho Journals*, she skipped out on witnessing Delgado's exhumation of a body that had been in the ground for fourteen months, leaving us to observe it. This is what leadership is all about.

Dennis Rathbone had arranged conversations with Rocco Cavaletti and Carlos the driver for 10:45, so Cody and I drove out to the mansion about an hour after she left. We were in Cody's small Ford.

"I still don't feel good about the cane," I said. "It would be different if I thought Miss Rachel had killed him."

"I know. But it's not about what we think or feel. It's about proper procedure, if you can stomach that. I know you're not big on doing things by the book."

"When I'm painting I inhabit a world where there are very few rules. You clean your brushes when you're done. You make your nude model feel comfortable if you're using one. You use high quality materials so the picture lasts for the buyer. Beyond that, you can do whatever you please. You can follow your instincts, and my instincts don't like this."

"I know, but at the end of the day this is partly about trust, and we need Delgado's ongoing trust to keep feeding us information on this and on future cases. Look at it that way."

I nodded. "But would he feel obliged to tell us

about the cane if our positions were reversed?"

"Maybe, maybe not. He showed us the x-rays and the autopsy photos, didn't he?"

"Sure," I said, "but he also likes to prove himself right when we're not, or show us up when we're not moving as fast as he is."

"Well, it doesn't matter as much to me *why* he does the right thing as *that* he does it."

"I can see that." There was no good answer to this. Five minutes later we pulled up to the gate, sat through twenty seconds of cameras scanning us, then drove up the slope and parked along the low stone wall that edged the parking area. Once inside, Rathbone led Cody off to his meeting with Carlos and I went upstairs to the small library off the lower terrace where I had talked to Celeste four days earlier. I didn't see anyone else as I went in.

CHAPTER TWELVE

While the temperature on the terrace would surely be more inviting in an hour or so, Rocco Cavaletti preferred to sit inside. It was a chilly morning as it can sometimes be at this altitude, even in July. He was much smaller than his brother, Luc, wearing designer jeans and a neon green form-fitting Nike training top. Trim and well muscled, he looked like he worked out regularly. I didn't assume that also meant he had no vices.

"So you're the detective," he said with an uneasy chuckle after we'd introduced ourselves. He was working his hands together but stopped short of cracking his knuckles. My impression was that he had not only failed to cultivate much refinement, he positively rejected it.

"I'm one of the detectives, the one whose name is on the door. Please have a seat."

"My Aunt Rachel told me you don't think Dad's fall was an accident."

He's ready to get this over with, I thought as I

nodded. "The police have x-rays and photos showing a set of injuries that couldn't have come from the steps."

"What do they think it was?"

"They don't know for certain. This case is still wide open. I'm hoping you can help us out."

"I can tell you what I know." He made a careless gesture with his left hand, as if to suggest that wouldn't be much. My eye caught his watchband, an organic pattern in red and black. Possibly lizard, I thought, and one of a kind.

Where Luc was blond with a light complexion, Rocco was dark with black hair and brown eyes. He looked like he might need to shave twice a day. I could already see a lack of patience in his manner and probably an absence of trust as well. But then, my questions were often unwelcome to a lot of the people I talked to.

"Let's start with where you were that evening, say between eleven and twelve P.M."

"I had already gone to my room. I always get up early and work out, so I never stay up too late."

"Is there a gym in the house?"

"No, but here I can jog instead on the road below the gate." As if his palms were moist, he rubbed both hands on his thighs.

"Did you see your brother that night?" Luc had told me he left at 9:30 for The Boardwalk.

"I only saw him at dinner. I know he went out

later, but I'm not sure when. The next time I saw him was out in the parking area after the police arrived. He came up in a taxi."

"Do you know where your father was after dinner?"

"I didn't see him. He might have been with Celeste. I guess you must know about her, I mean if you've been talking to everybody."

"Not enough. I've heard her name a few times. Tell me about her."

"She was with my dad. They were a couple, OK? Celeste was officially his secretary but there was a lot more going on with her than that." He laughed uneasily, not looking at me.

"How does your mother deal with that?"

"My mother mostly doesn't deal with anything because she doesn't have to. That's the way she has her life set up. She sits in her room, which at home is more removed, almost like in a separate wing, and she sips gin all day. She's off the traffic pattern you could say; you'd never run into her by accident. By dinnertime she's incoherent, which is another reason for her not to come to the table. She would probably start throwing things at Celeste."

"That makes me wonder why she came along on this trip."

Rocco looked at me for a long moment. "I think

it's because Miss Rachel made her come. Miss Rachel acts the part of the old matriarch sometimes and she hates the idea of buying property here. She probably thought my mother could bring some pressure to bear against Dad."

"Could she?"

"I doubt it. If she had any real influence with him she would've used it for other issues, and long ago."

"Are you active in the wine business?" I was thinking about Luc's comment.

An impatient look came over Rocco's face as if this were a direction he didn't wish to pursue. "Not much. Luc was always the takeover guy. It'll be even worse now with Dad gone."

"What do you mean?"

"Luc's always been Mister Know-it-all. He's been grooming himself to run the business for years. And you know what's really funny?" He leaned forward about six inches and his voice dropped in volume.

"What?" I said. Rocco wasn't laughing.

"Luc and my dad were not related, OK? He had a different father than I did."

"I don't understand that. I thought your parents had been married for more than thirty years."

"Right, but I got a sample of Dad's and Luc's DNA and had them tested at one of those places online. It came back marked 'no relationship.' My dad was not his father.

I had always suspected that, just from his looks. I ought to be sitting where he is, but that won't ever happen."

I could only stare at him for a moment. His face now held a satisfied smirk. In this business I've come across people who cultivate their victimhood; they nurture it to give them a sense of moral superiority. I wondered whether Rocco might also be in this group.

"Does anyone else know this?"

"Well, my mother must know it. I wouldn't be surprised if that was her little joke on Dad, after all his screwing around."

"But you haven't mentioned the DNA test to anyone else?"

"No."

"What was your relationship with your father?"

He shook his head. "Better ask someone else that. He didn't have a lot to say to me. Even as a little kid my job was always to try to be as good as Luc. I don't think Dad ever thought I was made of the right stuff. My style has always been more like coach in a family that travels first class."

"Where did you go to school?"

"I had a year at Berkeley in political science. After that I took some time off. It wasn't a good fit." Eight years off, to be precise, I thought.

"Was your father having any conflicts with anyone that you know of?"

"There's been a really strong undercurrent between him and Miss Rachel all through this trip. You could feel it any time they were both in the same room."

"This was about whether to acquire some property here?"

"I think that was most of it. Two days after we got here he asked both Luc and me if he could count on our vote if it came to that. We both own ten percent of the company."

"What did you say?"

"I said I would, and so did Luc. But our votes wouldn't be enough to let him borrow the money to do it, it would only work if he could come up with enough without going to the bank, then it would be fine."

"What percentage of the votes would he have needed to borrow the money?"

"In the corporation papers it says he had to have two-thirds."

"So both the two forty percent owners would have to agree. Without one of them he couldn't have any more than sixty percent."

"Right."

"But wouldn't there also be the larger issue of development then? Building the facility, planting and nurturing the vines. Paying for all that labor for years before the first bottle even ships? It would be a long time before the new property had any positive cash flow."

"I suppose. I'm not much of a business head."

"Are you working a regular job?"

Rocco looked away with a smile that must have been meant only for himself. "I guess that would be my full time position as a member of this family. They pay me a decent salary for that. And I get ten percent of the profits too."

I didn't ask how much that was, but my growing sense was that it wasn't enough.

CHAPTER THIRTEEN
CODY WILLIAMS

Cody watched Paul head up the fatal stairs before he went off with Rathbone to the interview with Carlos Fuentes, the house driver. They crossed the elevator vestibule and passed through an unmarked doorway leading to a corridor on the same level. At the far end a pair of French doors opened into the courtyard.

"You shall have the same table you used when you spoke with Ximena," Rathbone said, looking around as they approached it through a cluster of palms and paused at the base of a huge yucca. No one else was in view. "Now that's odd. Why don't you have a seat and I'll locate Carlos. I know Carmela told him to be here." He looked at his watch and shook his head.

Cody sat down at the cast iron table on a matching chair, took out his pocket notebook, and flipped through it. He had little information on the driver, although his impression was that it was odd for him to be late for this interview. Carlos was twenty-three years old, and his marital status had not appeared in Cody's information. Might he still have a romantic interest in Ximena that survived, even if derailed for a time by her incident with Sebastian? The kitchen helper had vaguely confirmed something of that kind, although in her efforts to conceal what happened with Sebastian, she had also offered a contradictory network of improbable distortions and outright lies. It's difficult to read between the lines of a maze, Cody thought, also glancing at his watch. It was five minutes before eleven.

His eyes scanned the two levels of bedroom suites on the three sides of the courtyard above. A single housemaid moving between rooms was the only person visible. In his mind he went down the list of family and staff. No one stood out as a suspect more than the others. Like Paul and Maya, he did not put any faith in the idea that Miss Rachel had killed Sebastian. Celeste also seemed like an unlikely prospect, since she stood to lose so much more than she would gain. Paul's report on Luc offered no overt reason to suspect him. Rathbone seemed almost least likely of all, yet his whereabouts on the night of the murder was unclear. Perhaps Paul would turn up something from his conversation with Rocco Cavaletti. Cody's overall sense was that there remained layers and layers to go through.

And Elizabeth Cavaletti—was she the impossible choice she appeared to be? Surely she had a motive, since she would inherit the forty percent of the family winery her husband owned, and she must be deadly tired of Sebastian's constant philandering. How many private secretaries had there been before Celeste? The life Elizabeth had created for herself was partly a fiction to avoid having them constantly in her face, and partly a way of elevating her personal martyrdom to legendary status. Still, having said that, her physical capabilities were impossible to assess.

Rathbone reappeared, winding his way among the plants and ponds. "I can't explain this, sir, but we don't seem to be able to find Carlos at the moment. He doesn't answer his cell."

Cody studied his bland expression in order to match it. "What do you think that means?"

"It is not part of my job to speculate on such matters, sir, but I am already distressed by his failure to appear, since I was charged with setting up this meeting. Please accept my apologies." Other than a clenched appearance to his chin, Rathbone's face showed little other emotion.

"Should we do a walkthrough of the premises together? Could he be hiding somewhere?"

"Perhaps, but first, please wait here a moment longer while Carmela and I go through the staff quarters. Its possible that one of the maids has seen him."

"You might talk with Ximena too," Cody

suggested.

When Rathbone did not acknowledge this, Cody nodded, knowing that Rathbone's proposal was only a polite way of saying the staff would prefer to do a further search without his assistance. That was fine with him. The household employees all had some degree of credibility riding on this, and he felt certain they would not help Carlos avoid this conversation if that was what was happening.

Another fifteen minutes passed, during which Cody had gone through the alibis of all his possible suspects more than once and was now shuffling the potential NFL rankings for the coming season. He found this more productive. At least, aside from the draft picks, all the players had a prior pro record to feed into his calculations.

Down the path and under the thick foliage a sudden veiled movement caught his eye. A flash of blue cloth, a shirt, perhaps, was slipping along beneath the broad leaf philodendrons and the sago palms that branched out close to the ground. Carlos' driver's uniform was blue. For an experienced detective, stealth is a larger red flag than anything else could ever be. It can only mean one thing. No stranger to stealth himself, Cody rose and slipped behind the thick trunk of the yucca. This would not be Rathbone trotting up with an urgent message.

Since he had no time to make a careful analysis

of what was happening, instinct took over. At sixty-three, Cody was no longer as swift as the coming sprinter, but was nearly twice his size. Experience counts for something too, as does sheer mass. As the fleeing suspect flashed into the cleared space edging the table, Cody reached out with both his foot and his hand, tripped the runner into a sprawl even as he seized his collar and yanked him to a halt. The kid was both dazed and shocked.

"Carlos," Cody said in Spanish, "thanks for stopping by. We need to talk now. Sit down." By his armpits he lifted the squirming driver upright from the stone pavers and set him on a chair near the table. "Take a moment to compose yourself. If you make a sudden move, I'll put you on the ground, much harder this time." He lifted his left arm so Carlos could see the profile of his shoulder holster. Breathing hard, the kid leaned back in the chair and tried to calm himself.

It was two or three minutes before Cody spoke again, letting the tension build. He kept both hands before him, open and ready. "I was sorry to see you running like that, Carlos. Usually it means you've done something bad. In this case, that would be the murder of a very important man in his community back in California. He was a guest in San Miguel. The police here are deeply sensitive to crimes like that, because the American authorities get so rude about it." He waited for this to sink in. Privately he doubted that Diego Delgado cared much about the American authorities, although he did get pressure now and then from the mayor, who had a greater sensitivity to public relations. "You are lucky that I know Licenciado Delgado of the police so well. We are like close friends. I would be able to say a good word for you when you are arrested for murder. Of course, whether I decide to do that depends on how well you cooperate with me now. This is the time to make a difference in what you know is coming. You will look back on this moment later, how it went because of your decision. Did you kill the señor in self-defense? That would make a difference."

"That man was scum, a piece of *basura* (trash) on the street, a bag of shit thrown from a car window." Carlos leaned over and spit into the red tufted blooms of the bromeliads at the edge of the path.

"OK, so now we can see that you had a motive." Cody was nodding with encouragement. "What else? What did you hit the *señor* with so he would fall down the stairs?"

Carlos folded his arms tightly against his chest and stared darkly into the foliage.

"I want to remind you of something. This is your best opportunity to explain what happened. You should understand that we have already talked to Ximena."

This provoked a spark. "She would tell you nothing of her shame!"

"That was not the case. I think she was trying to protect you by taking some blame on herself."

"He should go to the *carcel* (jail). He was a criminal for what he did to her."

"Possibly, but so is someone else in this house. If it's not you, then you need to tell me who pushed Señor Cavaletti down the steps. I think you know who it was, if you didn't do it."

Here Cody felt it was appropriate to give Carlos an encouraging smile, if only a subtle one, to suggest that all was not lost and not everyone had turned against him. But this was the same moment that Carlos chose to lift the edge of the cast iron table with both hands, and placing his shoulder under it, upend it over onto Cody, knocking him backwards in his chair beneath it. By the time Cody had scrambled to free himself, Carlos was long gone, sprinting through the corridor to the elevator vestibule and out the front door.

A little dazed himself, Cody shook himself after he crawled out from under the table and staggered onto the path. His knees and elbows were badly bruised and he suddenly felt stiff all over. A bump was growing on the back of his head and the edge of the table had imprinted a second cleft on his chin at a right angle to the first one. Was age catching up with him? He had no hope of overtaking Carlos and he steadied himself with one hand against the wall near the corridor. By the time he reached the front steps outside he was only somewhat recovered.

But being somewhat recovered did not prepare him for the scene in the brilliant sunlight of the parking area as he limped out the door.

CHAPTER FOURTEEN

When I came out of the house the first thing I saw was that the third act of our investigation had run off the rails. Cody was nowhere in sight. I assumed he was still tied up in his interview with Carlos. Two expressionless policewomen were guarding Miss Rachel in a wheelchair, both facing her as if expecting a violent move. She gripped a cane that was lying across the armrests, but it was a standard wooden version with a black rubber tip and a rounded over handle at the top. She was not looking in my direction and I didn't care to see the expression on her face either. At least she wasn't handcuffed. One of the matrons held a businesslike leather purse that had to belong to Miss Rachel.

This was the outcome of Maya's goodwill trip downtown to tell Delgado about Miss Rachel's collector cane. It went far beyond what we had feared could be the result of her visit, but you could also never predict what Delgado would leap at. Knowing the new suspect as I did, Delgado must have felt desperate. Sometimes he came under varying degrees of pressure by nameless sources from above that he would never talk about to us, and in the past the outcome had occasionally been an erratic move like this one. Usually that was the only aspect of it we ever saw. I also understood after many encounters in the past that what might look to us like erratic behavior may have made perfect sense to him. He never came on with great dignity, but he also had a small appetite for rudeness. Naturally, Miss Rachel's brusque and condescending manner would've offended him from the outset.

Standing off at some distance, Diego Delgado now held her Jack London cane in his latex-gloved hand like a scepter or an ancient sacred object. A plastic bag had been secured over the handle with a length of official string from which hung a tiny tag. An ambulance waited ten feet away with the rear doors open and the motor running. Two male officers in black bulletproof vests and sunglasses watched the scene in silence, hands on their guns. Rathbone stood helplessly between them, his arms folded. His face was as close to expressing strong emotion as I had ever seen it.

I was still frozen on the front steps considering whether to go back inside and locate Cody to witness this scene, when at that moment he staggered out of the vestibule behind me looking like he'd come off second best in a bar fight near closing time. His chin was bruised an ugly violet on one side. He was rubbing both his elbows and muttering as he limped past me on his way to speak to Delgado. I followed close enough to hear what was said.

"Did you see a kid come running through here at top speed?"

"I saw Carlos Fuentes, but he wasn't running. He drove off in the Mercedes." Delgado pointed at the gate with the cane, handle outward, a way she never used it. As with Miss Rachel, he must have still found something gestural about it, as if it possessed the ceremonial power to influence events.

"You didn't try to stop him?"

"But for why, Señor Williams? Can't you see we have solved this case? We made an arrest. Now we are going downtown. The *señora* will have no further use for your services. You may prepare your final bill."

That would be up to her, I thought, but it still nearly made me laugh, not the proper response in the circumstances.

Cody turned to me with a look of rank disgust and frustration. The house had two cars as part of its equipment. One was a white Suburban used for airport runs and hauling people around in groups. The Mercedes that Carlos had taken, a white E350 model sedan, was for short distance runs with couples or individuals. Each had a small bronze-colored logo on the driver's door, a coat of arms within a laurel wreath. I had checked out both vehicles on an earlier visit, so we at least had the license numbers. The gate was set up to open automatically when a driver approached from inside the estate. Leaving at a normal pace, although his eyebrows must've gone up when he saw Miss Rachel under arrest, Carlos was long gone.

I desperately wanted to hear what had happened to Cody inside, and why he needed to collar Carlos. Although from his injuries I could imagine some of the grounds, instead I turned slowly to face Miss Rachel Cavaletti, our client. *Our client*, now about to be hauled off to a Mexican jail and held without bail as she awaited her trial for murder. As I met her outraged gaze, I was counting the number of synonyms I could come up with for *stupid*, the only way I could describe our present course of action. To call it feeble-minded would've been a compliment. It reminded me of a few tough times when I had faced my mother as a child, times when I had no possible excuse for what I had done. Times that perfectly defined the essence of faulty logic.

I also thought of it as unintended consequences, but if I brought it up again, I knew Cody would still say we had done the right thing, and it was only Delgado who had acted foolishly in reaction. This was fine as far as it went, but shouldn't any decision like the one we made need to consider Delgado's potential reaction? This had been like making a chess move without considering the other player's position.

"I just cannot imagine how this could ever have happened," Miss Rachel hissed, bent over her dime store cane, her voice as acid as old vinegar. "Do the people here have no damn idea at all who they're dealing with?"

"Well, that would be part of it, I'm sure, if they didn't," I said. "They mainly drink large bottles of beer and cheap vodka or tequila. Some of them have never tasted wine. The other thing, and I need to tell you this now, is that your cane handle is a close match for the injury on the back of Sebastian's head. But so is the fireplace poker from the great room."

She looked back at me as if, even at my age of forty, I still lacked the ability to distinguish between good and evil. That idea may have had some merit as we stood there. "Isn't it obvious to them which one it was?"

"They think so, but it's not what you might say."

Cody came hobbling up as if one of his knees was not working right. He had been close enough to catch some of this. "But here's a question, Miss Cavaletti. Do you always have that cane in your possession? Like, specifically, when you go to bed do you take it into the bedroom with you and close the door?"

"Well, much of the time I don't remember it. It's usually next to my chair at the television, or staying here,

I've normally been setting it at the end of the sofa. I don't strictly need it to get around, you know. It's more of an aid, like if my balance is a little uncertain." She looked at him as if he might easily understand this. It made me think of the long staircase.

"Then when you get downtown that's the first thing you need to say to Delgado," I said.

"But why? I know that someone on the household staff must have killed Sebastian." Cody and I were both silent at this. It was possible, even likely, but we weren't ready to announce it. Delgado chose that moment to rush over.

"And you believe he was killed with the poker?" Cody said.

"No!" Delgado yelled. "No! That is enough for the Zacher people! Go back!"

"Why?" I said in a more rational tone.

"You must not talk to her anymore. She is mine!"

With an abruptly spasmodic effort, Miss Rachel reached into her waistband, pulled out a business card, and placed it in my palm. The policewomen both moved in to pull her arms back.

"This is my attorney. Call him now! Tell him what happened. I need him down here at once!"

As they wheeled her away I didn't have a chance to say that he couldn't practice law in México and that he would not be likely to even know what the law governing her situation was. Of course, he would have to associate himself with some local criminal attorney. One of the officers was advancing on us with a sweeping motion of both hands so Cody and I moved off.

The two policewomen and the two bulletproof officers lifted Miss Rachel, still in the chair, into the ambulance, pressing her head lower into her chest as if in humility to be allowed through the doors. Like that was ever going to work with her. Whoever was tangling with Miss Rachel down here had better be fully armed and dangerous.

"Her lawyer's name is Mark Savio," I said to Cody, reading from the business card, "of Savio, Denton, and Barwick. The office is in San Francisco on Montgomery Street. Sounds like he's the senior partner. I'll call him as soon as we get home."

As we watched Delgado's people wrap up the scene, Cody told me about his brief but dramatic meeting with Carlos. When I asked if he needed any attention to his injuries he impatiently batted the question away. After all, he'd been shot on four prior occasions in Illinois. And they say México is a dangerous place.

Twenty minutes later, when we pulled up at my house, I was understandably driving Cody's Ford. He had run the passenger seat back as far as it would go and he'd been massaging his knees most of the way. I thought of suggesting what Celeste might do for him, but held that back. Inside I found a flexible ice pack we kept ready for such moments and we settled in the loggia while he moved it around on his injuries. I sat down at one end of the table with a notebook and called Mark Savio's office.

Of course, he was in a meeting. My watch said it must be about 9:30 A.M. there, two hours earlier, since we're on Central time in San Miguel. In unemotional terms I briefly told the secretary the story of Miss Rachel Cavaletti's arrest in México on the flimsy grounds of the shape of her cane handle. Thirty seconds later Mark Savio flew out of the meeting and was on the other end of the line. I introduced myself and described our position in Miss Rachel's situation. He already knew Sebastian was dead and that the local police had decided it was a murder.

"OK, say your name again? I'll be down there by tomorrow evening. I'll get my own local legal crew set up in San Miguel but I'll want a detailed briefing from your agency the following morning, say in forty-eight hours. Is that possible?"

"Of course. Call me at this number when you get in tomorrow night."

"Give me the contact information for this Delgado guy. I assume you have it?"

I gave it to him.

"Is he the District Attorney?"

I explained that in this legal system he was like an ADA with investigative duties.

"And you're a private investigator licensed by what, the state there? Do they even have states there? What the fuck, you guys don't know who you're dealing with. Christ, what a nasty place for her to get busted!"

"Licensed? Nobody's licensed. This is México, in the state of Guanajuato. Anybody can do anything here. Relax, we're just snoops, but we're good at it."

"But I'm sure you have insurance, right?"

"Why? If anything goes wrong here it's fate. Nobody sues anyone as a way of getting rich here. The lawyers do things like wills, contracts, and property transfers."

In the itchy silence that followed I could almost hear Savio scratching his head at this. I wondered what this phone call was costing Miss Rachel. She was paying for both sides of it.

Cody paused his elbow massage to listen. Talking to Mark Savio reminded me of how much my attitudes had changed in eighteen years of living in San Miguel. Was the San Francisco lawyer going to be more a problem than a cure? México is not a southern suburb of the United States; it's a somewhat distant neighbor, even though they share a border. Often the way things are done here suggests a greater distance than mere geography would indicate from that single meandering line.

There's both a mental and a stylistic difference between those cultures that can often be profound.

"And Miss Rachel hired you on that basis? That's not like her at all."

"We're the only detective agency in town. Initially she hired us to prove Sebastian Cavaletti's death was accidental."

"Good job on that, by the way. OK, I just wanted to know who I'm dealing with."

"You can check us out online. It's the Paul Zacher Agency." I spelled it out for him. I'd had a website guy work up a plausible webpage for us a few years before. As such things often are, it was a bit touchy-feely, but on the screen all three of us appeared upbeat and competent, especially Maya, without actually moving through the air in slow motion with our hair lifting in the breeze. I hadn't looked at it in a while. Maybe I should to see if my hair was really thinning a little, as Celeste had suggested. At least the website had a contact button and we'd gotten a couple of decent cases from it.

Although I hadn't expected him to invite me up to join him in the Bohemian Club or for lunch at the Fairmont, signing off with Mark Savio was brief and somehow awkward. I felt I'd failed to sell him on both our competence and our commitment to the Cavaletti case. So far it had not been our most successful effort, but the early and middle phases of many cases often look quite similar in their shared bleak and unproven expectations. At least that part had a familiar feeling.

Maya had come downstairs during this call and was treating Cody with her special kind of affectionate medicine. He'd been in love with her for years; that was no secret, and he was recovering rapidly under her magic touch. I had a sudden image of Celeste working on Sebastian, except that Maya never did more than tease Cody. It was always flattering for her to have a man who worshipped her waiting in the wings in case I was killed in a case.

"So now they busted Miss Rachel," she said, always the expert on American slang. "I had a bad feeling about that when I left Delgado's office. He had a certain gleam in his eye that I had seen before. Is she now between the sword and the wall? Or are we?"

"A little of both, probably. Cody can tell you about his encounter with Carlos the driver." He was already nodding in a gentle way that didn't aggravate his principal injuries.

"That explains his wounds," she said. "Poor darling. Is Carlos a boxer?"

Cody's story included a few painful details that had not been part of the narrative he gave me, but I understood that. After all, unlike Maya, I had not been kissing his neck as he related the incident in the car. This can be a harsh and unforgiving business, one that generates little gratitude and not a lot more money, so I did not be-grudge Cody those small but highly personalized perks. They usually count for more than their actual weight on the scale of often-chancy outcomes.

CHAPTER FIFTEEN

Two days passed in limbo while Licenciado Delgado barred us from contacting our client, under the inflexible judicial rules of the republic, as he said. His hands were tied. Hearing this, I pictured him in a typical revolutionary costume, with a blue tailcoat and a three-cornered hat. In the interim we heard nothing more from Mark Savio except that he would meet us at our house at 9:30 on the morning after his arrival. I had already given him the address along with our sparse list of qualifications. If the truth had to be told, none of us even thought of qualifications anymore, and if we ever had, I couldn't recall those times. Daily reality was enough of a hurdle, and no certificate exists that could dependably take us over it. My dad used to call this The School of Hard Knocks. I knew even in childhood that the phrase was a cliché, but I never realized until we started the Agency what it really meant.

During this welcome lull, I started a still life painting without much hope of finishing it. What I mainly wanted was to finish this case and do more painting, and that didn't seem likely either. Probably less so. I could at least take some solace in the fact that new and hopefully competent players were soon arriving on the scene. They would surely possess some qualifications in the law that we did not. But had it now come down to a game about accreditation, where reality and experience didn't matter so much? If so, I was reminded that Mark Savio had never worked in México before, as far as I knew. In the credential-validated world he operated in, he would've brought that up if he had, and that gave me less confidence in him than before. México is not a quick study for any American, even those living here, and while being a highly paid San Francisco lawyer with an office in the Barbary Coast district may have evoked a bracing whiff of Melvin Belli in his day, it was not about to open a single door down here. Savio was going to need an expert counterpart from San Miguel to make any headway with Delgado, who had the broad experience of having come up against all of them in the past and more than once for those that mattered.

As far as a risk of prosecution for Miss Rachel, I couldn't see what evidence Delgado could've come up with. By itself, the antique cane head was as equivocal as the poker. A toss up will not get you a conviction, even here. She had either been present at the scene or not, another toss up, since no witnesses had come forward.

For the meeting on that Thursday morning, the ninth day of the case, we were all present at my house on Quebrada. Cody was a little more upscale than usual in a pressed white shirt and a suede sport coat with only a single tiny salsa stain on one lapel. Aside from a few issues with raising and lowering himself in the chair without grunting, he seemed close to normal. Maya was wearing a flattering summer weight cotton knit dress in a solid light green color, rather than her sprayed on jeans, and I had found a decent pair of chinos in the armoire that I hadn't worn since the memorial service for one of our clients earlier in the year. To counter this, I was anticipating something from the Armani summer collection from Mark Savio.

Instead when I opened the door I found him in designer jeans and a denim jacket over a pale solid color silk shirt. His embroidered cowboy boots had probably cost him a thousand dollars apiece. Perhaps he had been in México before, but only at the beach. He also carried a small pigskin document case on an adjustable shoulder strap. It looked like it would be a great deal more valuable than any document inside it.

He introduced himself as the woman behind him followed him in. "And this is my interim secretary, Celeste Howard. I think you may have already met her." I shook both their hands, hers quite delicately. Following him out of his view, she gave me a crafty look as I brought them inside. Five steps in, Celeste had already made me feel like we shared a secret, and although I couldn't recall what it was, she was certainly someone you'd want to have secrets with. She was wearing a jersey print wrap dress with a vee neck that suited her well even as it still managed to appear fairly businesslike.

Mark Savio was tall and elegant, with a sculptural crop of wavy, prematurely white hair that gave him almost an eloquent senior rock star look. The effect was Hal Holbrook meets Mick Jagger. With a Hawaiian tan that set off the hair nicely, he may have been fifty. We settled in the loggia at the edge of the back garden. I made the introductions and Maya brought out a tray with coffee and water.

As we got started, the feeling around the table was slightly awkward. Savio's law degree meant nothing here, and our position as experienced investigators in San Miguel meant nothing where he came from. Our only connection was that we both served the same client, if with varying degrees of success; but then, he hadn't tried yet. I had no idea about his background, but I already knew it would be useful to have a collateral degree in ambiguity to do business down here. Mexican Spanish has ten different words for it. I'm sure it hadn't been offered at his law school.

"I guess you may have had some initial concern about our credentials," Cody said, as if laying the groundwork for what was to come. "In case that's still an issue, I want you to know that I spent thirty years as a homicide detective in Illinois before we started the Paul Zacher Agency. Nothing has come up here so far that we haven't been able to handle."

I thought this overstated our success rate quite well. Handling means more than that we survived, but less than that we'd won every time.

Savio smiled neutrally. "And how many cases have you had?"

"This is our seventeenth," Maya said, still subtly studying Celeste, who was looking brightly around the table at each of us as if she felt she was the glue that held this meeting together. Taking in the way Celeste's dress clung to her, I was reminded of my comment to her in Sebastian's bedroom: "I guess we're all naked under something."

"And you consider seventeen cases to be a lot?" Savio raised the cup to his lips. His eyebrows lifted in surprise that the coffee was that good. Should I tell him that México is where coffee grows? What did he already know? What did he care to know? I didn't know.

"It seemed like a lot of cases at the time," Cody said in a level tone as if to lay a foundation beneath this conversation. "Each one came with its own obstacles. Sometimes it was only other people that were determined to get in our way. I've found that few of them genuinely want to help. When I run into someone who does, his stock goes up a whole lot. Right away I start looking for ways I can help him out too. Knowing this culture as we do, we can be *very* helpful." Both his eyes and his smile held a brittle glitter.

"It's lucky that we have Celeste to give us some insight into the reason the Cavalettis are here," said Maya. "I mean, being so much a part of the family, as she recently was."

Celeste looked around carefully for a moment as if she thought she might be about to step into something that could stain her shoes. "Well, of course. I was Mr. Cavaletti's secretary for the last three years of his life. So much of the winery business passed through my hands. It was hard not to know what was going on."

This defined her role with a sense of finality. She would be difficult to upstage.

"Strong hands they are, too," I added, nodding in encouragement. Mine no longer throbbed.

"If possible," Maya said, seeing an opening, "we would like to look at a copy of Mr. Cavaletti's will."

Savio looked surprised. "I imagine that may be possible, but we have never represented Sebastian Cavaletti, only his Aunt Rachel." When none of us responded, he continued. "What I want to know is how we can get Miss Rachel released from jail. At her age, she's very delicate. I'm not sure that law enforcement here will fully appreciate that, or act on it if they do."

Delicate like a rhinoceros facing horn poachers, I thought, recalling our conversation where she said how important it was to have someone around who would tell her the truth. How did Savio fit in with that, or was it only to people like us that he lied?

"I assume you're in touch with local counsel?" said Cody, always the moderate in scenes like this, at least initially.

"Yes, but we haven't had a chance to meet with them yet. I wanted to confer with the Zacher Agency first because you've been involved in this case since the morning after Mr. Cavaletti's death. I feel like I got onto this rather late in the day."

"Who are you using on this end?" Maya asked.

"I'd rather not say. I haven't mentioned your names to them either." He finished his coffee and edged the cup slightly forward for more, even though he didn't go as far as tapping on the rim.

"While we have a longstanding working relationship with Licenciado Delgado," I said, "it does not extend as far as him bending any rules governing an arrest for a charge like murder. Several of our clients have been arrested before, and he's never been willing to alter any of his established procedures. We can certainly fill you in on all the details we uncovered as the case developed, but as for the legal aspects of it, we'll have to recuse ourselves." I thought that was a nice, round, legal word to use with him, one he had heard many times. I couldn't recall ever having an occasion to use it before.

"OK, I can see that," said Cody. "Besides, the criminal code in the state of Guanajuato has changed recently and we're not up to speed on any of the detail of it, although I did hear that accused people are no longer guilty until proven innocent."

Mark Savio looked at him for a long moment. "Well, that's a break, isn't it? Too late to help Marie Antoinette, of course, but I suppose it was based on the Napoleonic Code before."

I shrugged, not wanting to tell him that Marie Antoinette preceded Napoleon on the stage of history. Savio could earn his fat hourly rate by researching it, or have Celeste do it. "If you like I can tell you what we've learned so far based on our conversations with the family and staff people."

"Of course." He nodded at Celeste, who produced a tiny voice recorder from her purse and set it in the center of the table. This level of restraint was a side of her I hadn't seen before. Savio picked up the recorder to announce the date and location, then named all the people present.

I identified myself and started by going through everything we had learned about the crime, including the x-ray and photo information from Delgado, the configuration of the surface injuries to the victim, and a description of Miss Rachel's cane and the fireplace poker. I included nothing subjective from our interviews, only the details of whereabouts, time frames, and relevant comments. Maya and Cody did the same for people they had talked to.

"Have any of you come up with a conclusion about who might have killed the victim?" Savio said when we'd finished.

"For my money," said Cody, "it was Carlos Fuentes, the driver, in revenge." He had already covered the strong implication of Sebastian's sexual abuse of Ximena in his review of their conversation.

"What was Delgado's response when you stated that to him?"

"We didn't get a chance to mention it in any detail," I said. "When we came out of the house Carlos had driven off in the Mercedes, fleeing from Cody, and Delgado was convinced he had solved the case by arresting Miss Rachel. He wasn't interested in hearing anything more from us."

"I see. And that's where we still stand two days later." Savio said this as if with a heavy heart. I thought this emotional component was overdone. Certainly he couldn't have done that in court without an objection from the other side. Was the implication that we'd been sitting on our hands? I was relieved that he hadn't asked how Delgado knew about Miss Rachel's cane. But for us to speculate would've been of little use to him, since he didn't know we had given Delgado that information. He could ask Delgado himself if he needed to know how he got it. It still seemed to me that the fact that Delgado now knew about it was the main point.

"What now?" said Celeste, in a less than secretarial tone.

I tried to read her in this new role, but got nothing. Surely part of the rehearsal had come from her background in Sebastian's business life.

Mark Savio took the cue. "We need to establish a consistent link so that I can know what you know, all of you. I'm thinking of a regular end of day report by cell phone. If you don't have anything you can just tell me that, and if something important comes up earlier, then I want to be notified immediately." He looked around the table. "Anything else? Otherwise I think that's all."

"There is one thing more," Maya said. "We have now gone beyond the initial retainer by about eight hundred dollars."

"Of course." He handed Celeste the document case. She dug into it in a familiar way and pulled out a checkbook.

"How much will take us forward from here?" she said to Maya.

Maya gave her a charming smile that may have shown slightly too many teeth. "I think three thousand dollars would do it this time."

"To the Paul Zacher Agency?"

She nodded. Celeste made out the check with a fountain pen and a bit more flourish than was necessary, then handed it to Mark Savio for his signature. He signed it with a casual scribble and passed it across to Maya. Although I had been thinking about how to paint his hair all through this conversation, I was now regarding it as arrogant, if hair can be thought of as arrogant. It was the kind of hair you would use either for a television weatherman or a politician running for the Senate in a district where retired women voters predominated.

"That will do it then, I believe." With a curt nod Savio rose and turned back toward the house, where he struggled for a moment to decide which of three possibilities was the best way to enter. When Cody and I said goodbye, Maya took the lead and brought them inside to the foyer, and then to the front door. I watched the body language of Mark and Celeste. Although he'd only arrived the evening before, I thought it implied more of a connection than legal business strictly required. Perhaps she had decided to be very frank with him. I could believe it. Being a legal secretary in a top San Francisco law firm might fit her agenda well, even though I knew she liked to sleep in.

As I turned to collect the coffee tray and the cups I spotted Orlando, our long tailed garden grackle. By instinct he had chosen a cagey spot under the bromeliads to watch this conversation from. He doesn't trust strangers. I recognized his look as he stepped out again onto the path. He was shaking his head slowly, rocking back and forth from one gray foot to the other, and the expression in his golden eyes was crimped and judgmental. Nothing good can come of this, he seemed to say, mark my words. Sometimes he acts too much like a character out of Edgar Allen Poe, and I'm sure he knows it.

When Maya and Cody returned a moment later we settled back in.

"Whatever we tell him, Mark Savio is going to do things his own way," Maya said. Her look was not quite neutral.

"To the degree that anyone can do things his own way here," I said. "That's not an approach that often works in traditional societies. You can't just bull your way through. But we still have to report to him and work with him."

"He'll end up trying to denigrate Delgado's qualifications and that will offend him," said Cody. "Then his cause will go right down the tubes. Delgado has already dealt with his share of huffy gringos."

"And this will make the second one in this case," said Maya, "because he's got one behind bars that's huffier yet."

"I don't see any way we can intervene to improve

this," I said. "It will take Savio a while to realize he ought to listen to us on how to modify his approach. All I can think of is that we focus on bringing in Carlos, although Delgado may not lock him up if we do."

"I asked Rathbone to file a stolen car report through the house manager," Cody said. "If we find Carlos they can at least hold him on that."

My phone went off as he said this. It was Delgado. We went through the usual pleasantries. His boys were both doing well at the university in Guanajuato. I wondered if Savio was already breathing down his neck and he needed something from us, although I couldn't think what that might be.

"The attorney of Señora Cavaletti is on his way here," he said. "As a courtesy I am calling to tell you about the cane before I tell him. Since at the beginning the information came from you. So helpful indeed it was."

"Really?" Was he gloating somehow? I wondered how he could've compared it closely enough to Sebastian's head injuries to make a choice between the cane and the poker. "Did you get something from it?"

"Caught under the edge of the metal, where it meets to the wood, we have discovered a human hair."

"OK, but human hair only has DNA in the follicle. Did you get that much?"

"No, unfortunately, it was broken off. But you will recall on the back and side of the victim's head we had shaved those areas of the injury. Naturally, we saved that hair sample and under the microscope this is a perfect match."

"Did you get any blood from it?"

"No."

I covered the receiver and sketched this in for the others.

"That's not enough to convict her in a capital case," said Cody, standing up with a slight grimace and placing his hands on his hips, "even here."

"So that is one piece of evidence to favor the cane as the weapon," I said into the phone. "I think the larger question is whether she had the cane with her at all times. She told me she often did not take it to bed with her in the evening. She would leave it leaning on the end of the sofa."

"Well, of course she would say that, even to me, as she did, and more than once. Anyone would in this situation."

"How about fingerprints?"

"We found only hers. But that says nothing too. Anyone else using that cane as a weapon would wipe it clean and put it back, if as you say, it was at the end of the sofa at the hour of the murder. Then she would pick it up again when she came out of her room and place new prints on it. Nothing could be more natural."

"So," I said, unable to disagree with any of this,

"then why did you decide she was the killer? She's an elderly woman. The victim was a family member. Just because the cane belonged to her, to me that's not enough. Anyone in that house could've killed Sebastian Cavaletti. Even any one of the staff who was not normally there at that hour but had a key could've come in and killed him." Thinking of Carlos as I said this.

"I know this, but I am not disturbed by it." His voice took on a smug tone.

"But think about motive! What motive would Miss Rachel have?"

"I will tell you this because as ever we are working so closely together, even if on opposite sides of this case."

This didn't sound good. "Yes? What else do you have now? Tell me!" By this point I was forgetting my Mexican manners, which I knew would probably cost me later.

"I have a copy of the will of the murder victim. It leaves his forty percent interest in the vineyard to his aunt, Rachel Cavaletti, in trust for his two sons equally upon her death."

"He bypassed Elizabeth!" I knew I was yelling.

"So you could say, thinking perhaps that in her difficult condition she could not manage the business even if she wished to. I would understand this kind of thinking even if she does not. Señora Elizabeth does receive his interest in their residence in California, which

180

is separate from the winery company, and most of his financial assets. At least his aunt had managed the vineyard in the past. Leaving it to her gives his boys a chance to mature before it goes to them. Do you see this now Señor Zacher how it goes?"

I did. I saw it go like a dark cloud drifting over our case and stalling out overhead. Next would come the torrents of rain that washed out all of our positions. My brain was spinning in place without even generating much friction.

"Any bequests outside the family?"

"Yes, several small charity amounts, and then two to individuals. His butler and his secretary each receive $50,000."

"Wait a minute! How did you get that will?"

In the moment of silence that followed I could almost hear Delgado drawing himself up to his full, five-foot-eight height.

"This document came from the private secretary of him, the Señorita Celesta 'Oward. I hope I have said this name properly."

"You have said it quite properly," I told him, rather coldly.

Certainly more properly than I would've said it at that moment.

CHAPTER SIXTEEN

This was not the first time I had felt that someone other than the Agency was pulling the strings on this case. If, as I had suggested to Delgado, the motive was the key, what would Celeste's motive have been for giving him the will? Was it merely her generous if somewhat impulsive frankness, for which she was now becoming legendary, at least in my mind? But was she not also a 'private' secretary to Sebastian in a number of ways? One thing this suggested was that she was not working that closely with Mark Savio, but then her revelation to Delgado must have occurred before the arrest, or at least before the lawyer's arrival. I began to feel that Celeste was playing a game here in which frankness was only one of her cards. Call it a face card, and probably the queen of spades.

After I brought Maya and Cody up to date and Cody had gone home, I put in a call to Rathbone. I was expecting his usual reticence. Certainly the most minute traces of adrenaline could never have been detected in his body, no matter what the crisis.

"Good morning, Rathbone."

"Good morning Mr. Zacher. What can I do for you today, sir?"

I had a sudden inspiration, not in what to ask, but how to ask it. "I have been conferring with Mr. Savio, and it occurred to me afterward that if something unexpected comes up, I might need to have a personal meeting with him on short notice. Do you have the name of his hotel? I may need to reach him quickly."

A brief silence followed. "Well, that is most convenient since he is staying here at the house with the family."

I was sure it saved them a lot of money on lodging expenses, although, like most other things, that would've been beyond Rathbone's range to speculate on.

"Not in Mr. Cavaletti's room, I hope."

This didn't ruffle him. "No, sir. Miss Howard is still using that room." I knew he had said this with an utterly straight face. Rathbone had intentionally sent me into her firm grasp. I sensed that he was playing a subtle game, but I couldn't make out yet what it was.

"And has Diego Delgado made any progress on the stolen Mercedes?"

"Not that I have heard, sir."

"Have you been in touch with him?"

"Yes, but he left me with the sense that the theft of a three-year-old vehicle, even if a Mercedes, was not his highest priority. He had, after all, arrested Miss Rachel for murder. He seemed to be riding on that, if you understand my meaning, sir."

He went on to confirm the family contact information for Carlos Fuentes, which we'd had earlier on the staff list.

"Is anything else happening there that you can share with me?" I was sure there were things that he wouldn't.

"Well, Mr. Zacher, there is one thing that might interest you in the Zacher Agency. Ximena has not returned to work since the arrest of Miss Rachel."

"She did not say why?"

"No, sir. Carmela has heard nothing from her. When she telephoned at Ximena's house they told her she was gone and they didn't know where."

I thanked him and said goodbye.

The next morning Cody and I started with a trip along the Cieneguita road, but I didn't expect to find Carlos at home, polishing the white Mercedes E350 in the front yard. On kilometer six we veered off to the left and wound around through a maze of rutted unpaved offshoots that had probably never had a plan more focused than charting a way through the trees and around the bigger rocks. It was raw, organic improvisation along the paths of least resistance. After asking for directions three times we found the house, a small three-room riverbed stone and concrete block affair on a winding lane with no name other than the street of the old Lopez family. The left end of the house was painted a dirty pink; the rest had never been painted at all, raw red brick oozing ancient dried mortar. Half a dozen chickens scratched the barren dry soil for the millionth time and the two aged dogs near the entry didn't bother to get up to greet us as we approached, although one lifted his head and yawned. This house was a step up from most others in the neighborhood. The two elderly women inside claimed to have not seen Carlos Fuentes in weeks. One of them had a cane but I didn't ask to examine it. Apparently Ximena's name meant nothing to them. Nor did ours.

This outcome didn't surprise me, but it was one of those tasks we had to do. Cody and I drove away in a frustrated but not surprised silence in his Ford. Maya had taken the van and gone riding, preferring the company of her Lusitano mare, Martina, to the kind of elementary grunt work we were doing. Before she left she had told me she didn't think that the answer to this case lay out in the campo—it was still inside that extravagant house. I didn't blame her. Her last words were, "Trust me. This is an impulsive rich person's crime."

Maya had come from a family with ample means in Mexico City, and while I appreciated her insight, it didn't offer me any specifics.

"You don't think it was Carlos Fuentes?"

"No, but that doesn't mean I know who it was."

Bouncing over the ruts, Cody and I had gotten back to the Cieneguita road before either of us spoke. At least it was paved, if ribbed with speed bumps.

"If it's only a matter of being on the run, Carlos could go over the border, as so many do," said Cody. "We've seen that before. I'm sure he's got some money, since working in a grand house like that, his pay would've been better than driving a cab. He may even have a car of his own. I can't imagine he'd be traveling in the Mercedes after fleeing like that."

"Going north is the anonymous solution," I said. "So that's a plus. We know the Mercedes has not been found. Once in Texas or Arizona he'd be part of a faceless labor pool. Going northwest into California, documents are not needed, or even desired. This time of the year (it was July) there's going to be a lot of fieldwork available. But that doesn't address why Ximena's gone missing. With her father's ongoing illness, she wouldn't be likely to leave him. To me, that suggests Carlos is still here."

Not much farther on we crossed the area in front of the train station. "Don't forget that flight can mean a number of things," I added.

"I'm focused on guilt as its principle meaning," Cody said.

"But you're still a cop in your own mind. That part never retires. Cops are always focused on guilt because sometimes it's pointless to arrest the innocent, although not always. But what if Carlos had a reflexive fear of pursuit? How about being blamed in the past and punished for something he didn't do? How about being twenty-three years old and he's never had a decent opportunity a single time in his life until this driver job? Then because of Sebastian's bad behavior, it blows up in his face, confirming everything he's always thought about his vulnerability to gringos and upper class Mexicans."

"Well, I'm not a cop anymore. Thirty years was more than enough."

"Still, most days you've got a cop's head on your shoulders."

"Here's what I think. Even if a Mexican guy like that will run when threatened with arrest, thinking he won't get a fair deal, he still attacked me when I was only sitting across from him at that table, which is not typically Mexican. I didn't attack him. He started it."

"You said you took him down sprinting when he tried to get away."

"Well, I didn't think of that as any more than a traffic stop where he was running a red light on foot."

"But how did he think of it? Anyway, why does that mean he's guilty? Flight is often only a reflex."

Cody did not respond to this, and it may have been that the most telling evidence we had against Carlos was that we didn't think Miss Rachel was guilty. Like the physical information from the cane, his flight was not enough to sway a jury.

I think of what followed as the no man's land phase of the case. Most of them have one. The dictionary defines this term as "empty because of fear or uncertainty." It offers no landmarks or watering holes, and no place to hide. No way to succeed. The trenches, when you find them, are full of spent shrapnel and dead things you don't want to think about.

Over the next four days we wandered the city of San Miguel looking not so much directly for Carlos, knowing that the police were not, but looking for Ximena or the Mercedes. Either one could be a link. I could think of no reason for the kitchen girl to leave her job except that she had patched things up with Carlos and gone into hiding with him. I still had the car's license number from my examination of both vehicles, but that was easy enough to change by simply stealing another pair. It might only have been switched, and since most people don't often look at their own plates, it might take a while to be reported. I couldn't imagine the police rushing to solve the case of the missing license plates. Most of the time, plates were lifted by the traffic police themselves for illegal parking offenses. Of course they didn't ever put a different set on in their place. Better than the plates, the key to identifying the Mercedes would be the small bronze logo on the driver's door.

Meanwhile, feeling like a faithful hired drudge, I called Mark Savio every night at nine o'clock to report our continuing defeat. He would never make any effort to report anything to me, of course. For him, any report recipient would've needed a legal credential of some kind. I began to wonder why he hadn't demanded to see my birth certificate and passport at our meeting. Although I had my college diploma somewhere, those were about the best things I had to offer in these document wars. Did the Paul Zacher Agency really exist outside my own mind?

CHAPTER SEVENTEEN

The following day I was standing in my second floor studio near the front wall of my house on Quebrada, where the glass is set back about a meter from the parapet, so that in looking down I can't see the sidewalk, crumbling mess that it is, or the parked cars, but I can see the street beyond. Loosening up the stiffened bristles of a thick brush, I was standing there trying to concentrate on painting, wanting only to start a picture even if I couldn't take it very far. I mainly wanted to prove that I still had a real life beyond what was feeling more and more like a dead end case. I had put on a CD of saxophonist Gene Ammons doing *Angel Eyes* to get me in the mood. A vehicle slowly pulled up, as if uncertain of the address, and paused directly on the cobblestones below, unable to find a parking place. I realized that I was looking at the top of a newish white Suburban very much like the one that belonged to the Cavaletti's rental estate. Even the luggage rack looked familiar, although I'd never seen it from this angle before. It had to be custom made, and most Suburbans don't have one like it.

As I watched, the driver's door swung open and Rathbone got out. I recognized him more from his uniform than from the top of this head. Had Miss Rachel's attorney come for a surprise visit? Or did the butler somehow believe he was coming to pick us up? I couldn't think why. At a measured pace he walked around to the passenger side and opened the rear door. I threw the brush down on my painting table, changed out of my painting shirt, and shut down the music.

"Maya! We have company." She wasn't in the bedroom or the bathroom and I found her downstairs in the kitchen. She looked up from the sink just as the doorbell rang. "It's Rathbone. He must be bringing Mark Savio for another conference with us."

"Wouldn't he have called first? Wouldn't that only be good manners?"

"Savio might be too lofty to think he needs any."

Maya pulled her apron off her shoulders and her hair off her face and we both went to the door. The Suburban was gone, so in that brief interval Rathbone must've found a place to anchor it slightly further down the street, no small accomplishment on Quebrada at any time of day.

There, supported on the arms of both him and the personal assistant, Elena, was Elizabeth Cavaletti with a look of grim determination (I won't all it stoic because the pain was dripping from her face like blood). Of course, I hadn't met her yet, but I'd heard Maya's dismayed description replayed several times, and the inch-wide band of our visitor's white hair moving left from her center part left little doubt who she was. She was wearing a loose black dress that came below her knees. It was a good quality fabric with a stiff look, as if it hadn't seen much action in public. Her shoes were also black and sensible with a Velcro fastener. It was a mourning outfit that she may have last worn at a funeral, and not recently. It also occurred to me that she might some day wear it at her own.

"Good morning, Mr. Zacher, and er, Señorita Sanchez," Rathbone said apologetically in an undertone. "Miss Elizabeth has discovered a sudden desire to see you. I apologize that we didn't have time to call first." I detected a note of controlled indignation in his voice. These were not his manners.

Elena stared at the pavement without comment. They weren't hers either. It occurred to me that Elizabeth hadn't allowed them to call ahead, hoping for an element of surprise. They all had cell phones that would've worked on the way as they drove in. Was she trying to catch us at something beyond simple unpreparedness?

"I just assumed you'd be keeping normal business hours," Elizabeth said with a sniff of dignity.

As if we were a grocery store or a gas station,

I thought.

"Perhaps in San Francisco, Mrs. Cavaletti, but this is a boutique business in México. We have never taken on more than one client at a time, and we don't ever see walk-ins, either. But please come in anyway." I was still wearing my painting jeans, which were not too badly stained with oil pigments, and I had pulled on a clean off-white sisal shirt from the Yucatán that went over my belt. Maya was dressed in her normal spray-on jeans, not the best pair she had by any means, and a dark blue cotton tee shirt that was an old favorite. On the back it said GODDESS. The white letters were cracked and faded from many washings, but they still made their point.

As Maya led us into the great room Rathbone leaned over to me and said, "Is there somewhere else that Elena and I might wait once she gets settled?"

I nodded. It was the now familiar Rathbone style of discretion, anticipating some kind of Elizabeth Cavaletti outburst as she chose a comfortable chair facing the fireplace. Above the mantel hung my portrait of Maya seated as Frida Kahlo. After Rathbone and Elena made Elizabeth comfortable I showed them out to the loggia, where they declined any refreshments. By the time I returned, Maya was facing Elizabeth with a welcoming look on her face but I could see she was more tense than when I left. Coming in, no one had introduced me, so I did it myself.

"And I am so pleased to meet you too," Elizabeth said. "I feel like we have been tiptoeing around each other for all this time since my dear Sebastian was so brutally murdered."

That must be the kind of tiptoeing that can be done without much strain from the center of a mattress, I thought. I knew from my notes and my daily reports to Mark Savio that we'd been on the case for only fifteen days. But from her statement she seemed to have moved her position forward a few squares on the board. Maya had noticed nothing in her earlier comments that included the idea of murder, so the information abut Miss Rachel's arrest must've come from Rathbone or the boys.

Although Elizabeth still appeared under strain from making this sudden public appearance, her expression was one of determination more than misery. Her hair was presentably combed and pinned into position with ordinary bobby pins. If it was not fashionable, it was at least subdued, even orderly, unlike her life. She wore no jewelry other than an engagement and wedding ring set in white gold. The stone and the setting were not ostentatious, probably paid for by a Sebastian Cavaletti then still in his mid twenties, and not yet a part owner of the vineyard. Even with a brilliant future awaiting him, he must have been only on salary.

"As I said then, I feel we were not able to completely finish our last conversation. Are you here about

Miss Rachel?" Maya said in her most diplomatic tone. She placed one hand over another on her knee.

"I guess nearly everything is about Miss Rachel these days, isn't it? That's why I made this great effort to come and see you."

"We appreciate that so much," Maya said, nodding too vigorously.

I knew she was now picturing the double margarita I'd be making for her later that day. The weather had recently been fairly humid, part of a rainy July, and tiny beads of moisture would be rolling down the sides of the thick greenish glass, suggestive of the inviting chill within.

As this developed I was thinking about how Maya and I hadn't had any chance to talk about how a meeting such as this might go. Even closely related to the family and the murder of her husband as she was, Elizabeth had never been our client. Arguably she was more connected to the core issue than even Miss Rachel. There was no way to ask whether she knew about the will, and I was not planning to bring it up.

We had tried to be sensitive to ethical concerns throughout this case, for example, Miss Rachel's cane and the debacle that caused, but how we would handle Elizabeth's unannounced appearance was far from clear or being anticipated. Yes, there was no more interested party than she was, but in hiring the Paul Zacher Agency,

Miss Rachel had authorized us to release no information to any third parties. It may have been our fault that it never came up, but the truth is that we had thought the boys would wait for the senior family members to keep them informed, and that Elizabeth would never leave her room. Maya and I now glanced at each other with the same thought, but we said nothing to interfere. Had we stepped in it again by not anticipating this encounter? Subtly, I checked my shoe soles for clods of dirt so that if I ended up kicking myself later I wouldn't leave any marks on my pants.

"So, recognizing how much it must have cost you personally to make this visit, how can we help you today?" I asked this as a modest prompt, not that she didn't already have her own self-directed agenda.

Elizabeth appeared to now consciously arrange an expression on her face that she had previously rehearsed. "I must begin by telling you how frustrated I am with the handling of this case so far." Her jaw took on a firmness beyond what I thought was possible from Maya's earlier description. It clearly implied the existence of some muscle tone.

"So are we," I said, sympathetically, referring to Delgado's belief that he had already caught the murderer. At least this was looking more like the family starting to pull together, an outcome we'd seen little of until now.

"Then why hasn't that horrible woman, that

witch, been brought to trial and convicted? Locking her up was only the first step! All I want is justice to be done for my dear Sebastian! The next thing that happens will be that Savio gets her released, probably by spreading bribes all over the police department here. That's how he works, you know, even at home."

Although neither of us has a degree in English, I like to think Maya and I can both still communicate well enough with English speakers. Here we only looked at each other blankly. This was a failure of psychology more than rhetoric or vocabulary. An unpleasant silence followed, where we, as the supposed experts in crime, had no easy response.

"I guess you haven't spent that much time in México," I finally said. "Have you even been here before at all?"

With the limp gesture of the long-term torture victim, she waved off any serious intent in this question. "I always read the newspapers that are brought to me; that would be enough for any intelligent person to understand what's going on here. The crime in this place is revolting and everybody gets off. This is why I tried so hard to persuade Sebastian to abandon the idea of starting a satellite vineyard here. Now this is the outcome of his foolish decision." She held out her hands palm upward to include our great room. As if to say, Who could ever explain this?

"Yet, I've lived here for eighteen years and somehow survived," I said mildly.

"And we've never paid a bribe to anyone," said Maya, "except an American cop once in Laredo when we went up there for some shopping."

Elizabeth's eyebrows went up. "And what did you learn from all those years down here? To keep your head down? Were you hiding under a table for most of that time?"

My blue eyes must've taken on an icy tone, and here I made a mistake. Hearing the truth spoken to her in a way that disregarded her long-running façade of being a helpless invalid was not anything she had experienced recently. I should have considered that I was not part of her hired staff. I wanted to say, "And where the hell have you been hiding for most of your life? Behind a case of gin bottles?"

Instead I said, believing I had toned down my response, "I want to remind you that in the Zacher Agency we represent Miss Rachel Cavaletti, not you." I noticed I had raised a finger toward her, so I folded it back against my palm. "If you have a problem with the way the police are handling this case, then I suggest you have Rathbone load you back into that Suburban and take you downtown. I have no influence over the police here, and you have no influence over the Paul Zacher Agency. Is there anything else you'd like to tell us? Because I don't think there's anything else we could tell you that you would ever listen to."

Her chin clenched and her lips curled in foul outrage. "Who in God's name do you think you are? You're just some small town hick detective in México, of all places on earth! I bet you got your skills from reading some cheap mystery novels. You're nothing but a predator looking for a meal ticket! Sucking that wretched old woman dry, murderer though she is, while she rots in a stinking Mexican jail. I'll bet they don't even give her any toilet paper. She deserves much better than that and so do I! I came here hoping to reason with you as an American! And yet all I get is your sarcasm and contempt, heaped on a woman who can barely walk upright, whose husband was brutally murdered within the last two weeks, and who was cut out of his will by that nasty scheming bitch they're holding in prison. Thank God at least for that much!"

"I don't think you can have it both ways," said Maya quietly, after a long moment of silence. "In this story are you the victim or is it Miss Rachel? Paul has to write this meeting up later and he will need to know."

"Of course I'm the bloody victim here!" If she had brought a cane (was it still in the Suburban?) she would've poked a hole in the tile floor with it. But I suspected Miss Rachel owned a prior claim on all the cane rights in that household. "I have always been the victim in this rotten family. No one cares a damn about me, and if I didn't stand up for myself, as hard as that is to do without crutches, then no one ever would."

Elizabeth had shown considerable vigor during this tirade, even to the point of waving her arms about as she yelled. Of course gin has a lot of calories, and her reserves may have been greater than we'd earlier estimated. By the time she wound down, sputtering, she was also shaking badly. Respectful witnesses that we are, we let her shake.

I had watched this performance with conflicted feelings. It gave me an intimate sense of day-to-day life in the Cavaletti winery estate in Healdsburg, California, and the violent undercurrents that must daily ferment there. The weight of decades of a frustrated and unfulfilling life was printed on her face, but her selection of us as her next victims to lash out at turned me off as much as it did Maya.

I knew Maya was angry at this outburst mainly for two reasons; she was insulted because it was happening so personally and uninvited in our home, and more generally, that it was not the way business is done in this country under any conditions. Elizabeth had disrespected her culture as well as her as an individual. I knew what I had to do.

"All right," I said with a calming gesture of both hands, palms downward. It was my voice of reason stance. "Let's all step back a space or two from this tone for a moment. Maybe taking a deep breath will help us reel it in a bit."

"Now you can just shut your mouth! How dare you speak to me like that! A woman who has been dragged through the living hell of misery that I have for two-thirds of her life! The unrelenting pain and psychological abuse, year after year, even as that nasty little tart still struts around the house every day wearing practically nothing. No wonder I am so rigidly confined to my room day and night! Wait until she's nearly sixty and let's see how good she looks then. She'll have to make room for her boobs in her pants pockets to keep them from bruising her knees."

This marked a distinct turning point because Maya cleared her throat and stood up, her face clouded over and threatening like the tropical storms from the northern Gulf of Mexico that sometimes lash us with their tail. Her hands were clenched into fists at her sides. "Excuse me," she said, her mouth hardly opening around her teeth, and left the room without looking at either of us again.

This brought about a short period of echoing silence, even though Maya had spoken softy. Now breathing hard, perhaps Elizabeth had only paused for an instant to catch her breath. I know I was trying to breathe normally, and I'd hardly had a chance to speak at all.

Any sense that I was moderating a rational discussion of issues of common interest to all of us was long shattered. The spaces in our great room were now piled so high with decades of Cavaletti family baggage that I could hardly see Elizabeth anymore.

Or perhaps that was only my wish.

Searching for a new direction, I found nothing more to add to this exchange. Although I could see Elizabeth was also groping for more logs to toss on the fire, her search for good tinder was interrupted by the return of Maya with Rathbone and Elena in tow. What had she said to them?

"I do fear that our parking time before the house has now run out," Rathbone said, glancing plausibly at his watch as he leaned over Elizabeth with a solicitous air. After all, few issues are less partisan than parking availability. Without knowing what Maya had told him, I was amazed at how skilled he was at defusing an ugly confrontation. But in that family, how much experience of this kind had he already had? I wondered if he'd trained for his present position in the diplomatic corps.

Adding no other comments, Elena and Rathbone both gripped Elizabeth by one arm and lifted her to her feet. I don't know if that was necessary, but they must've thought it was. I didn't want to question it. We walked with them to the entry at an invalid's pace, where only Maya and I and Rathbone said goodbye. He gave us a shaky smile that suggested they had been able to follow the progress of our discussion from the loggia. The scene was beyond any degree of composure that even he could fake. I did not close the door until they pulled out and drove away, but then I shut it quite firmly and threw the bolt home with a satisfying smack of steel on bare steel. Under my hand it felt like the end of a chapter by a writer who knows how to effectively wrap things up. I gently took Maya's hand as we walked back into the great room and we stood in silence before the fireplace for a long moment. When I put my arms around her she spoke.

"That was all about men, wasn't it? I could tell that she saw me as a victim too, probably the victim of your behavior, not that she knew anything about it."

"People make a lot of assumptions, and not many of them come from close observation." I said. Beyond that, I don't think either of us felt ready to comment further on Elizabeth Cavaletti's outburst. I wanted to sweep myself, or both of us, into a very small pile in a dark corner of the room while we thought about this encounter out of sight under calmer conditions. As ugly and misplaced as her eruption was, the genuineness of her pain was palpable and undeniable. This was the precise antithesis of the rosy portrait of Celeste and Sebastian drawn by the boys and Celeste herself.

As I pulled Maya closer against me I knew I also

wanted to have the upholstery cleaned on everything around us, starting with the chair Elizabeth Cavaletti had sat in to deliver her tirade. Have the Persian rug taken up and laundered. I wanted to bring Maya out to the thermal springs by the village of Atotonilco so we could both take a ritual steam bath as we flogged each other naked with birch boughs, although I wasn't sure where to find them in this part of México.

But what I wanted most was to forget we had ever met the Cavalettis. I was even ready to go back to drinking our old Chilean red. It was an honest working person's wine, somewhat above a jug wine, but one that had never been improved or infected with what the wineries called *noble rot.*

CHAPTER EIGHTEEN

We had reached a point in the Cavaletti murder case where nothing but silence surrounded us. We were hearing no new information from Delgado or Mark Savio, even though I spoke with the lawyer every evening. Sometimes it's at vacant moments like this that you can be granted a breakthrough. It's often nothing but luck.

Later on the day of Elizabeth Cavaletti's visit I stopped at the supermarket in the La Luciérnaga Plaza, our only large shopping center. Of course, it's not in the historic part of town, but up on the edge bordering the highway. Not everything here needs to really be seventeenth century or pretend to be.

I headed directly for the produce department, which is near the entrance on the parking lot side, in search of some lemons. After the ordeal of our confrontation earlier that day I found I was still muttering. It was not quite a string of obscenities, but instead a regurgitation of all the clever things I hadn't thought of to say in response to her that I was continuously coming up with now. Other shoppers were stepping out of my path with good reason. Most of us talk to ourselves but not so publicly.

The lemons weren't bad, just not as large as I liked and probably too full of seeds that would have to be fished out with a spoon after squeezing. I bagged up a dozen of them anyway. Maya would be looking for one of my margaritas tonight with the blend of lemon and lime in the mix that we both liked best. The asparagus was still looking good so I tossed a bundle of that into my basket. After locating a couple other items I got in line at the checkout counter behind three local women. I had stopped muttering by then and no one was paying attention to me any longer. That was a relief. I stood there as stiff as a post wondering if this was what ordinary, civil reality looked like. I have always been badly taken aback when someone acts with insane rudeness out of the blue. It has happened before. That's why I always avoid talking politics with other Americans.

The girl at the cash register was attractive and efficient. She wore the same green vest over a black skirt or slacks that they all did. When my turn came she gave me a brief conventional smile. I couldn't help noticing the paintable texture of her loose wavy hair. I glanced at her nametag because I like to use people's names whenever I can. It read Ximena Luz Altamirano.

My knees did not buckle and I was able to keep my face expressionless as I looked away, watching the packer at the end of the counter bagging my order. I had not met Ximena before at the house and there was no reason she would recognize me. A moment later I was headed for the parking lot as I fumbled for my phone. It was five minutes after five.

Cody had picked up by the time I reached the van. By then I was starting to react and my heart was pounding. This was the break that had so thoroughly evaded us. It was the fifteenth day of the case.

"I found Ximena."

"Ah, and if you found her we can probably get to Carlos. Where are you?"

I gave him the detail and we quickly developed a plan. It would be a simple stakeout. He planned to pick up Maya, they would meet me in the parking lot, and she would give me my gun and take the van home while Cody and I waited in his Ford for Ximena to get off work. Then she would lead us to Carlos and we would take him down. Turning him in to Delgado wasn't by itself enough to get Miss Rachel released, but at least he would be held in custody on the auto theft charge while we tried to gather more evidence on the murder.

It was a little chancy, but this still might be the beginning of the end: a tawdry narrative of sexual abuse committed by a man of high status against a young woman of low status, followed by a stealthy revenge with class overtones. It was also an old story, perhaps one of the oldest. We'd never had any high-minded murders on our case list. They were more often crimes you didn't want to talk about in polite company. No one kills for the best of reasons, only for the best reason they can think of at the moment.

Ten minutes later Cody's Ford pulled up next to me, and Maya got out quickly and got into the van. Cody stayed inside, not wanting to be seen in case Ximena emerged from the store. Maya handed me my gun inside a plastic grocery bag and I pressed her hand before I stuck it in my belt. An instant later she was driving away.

As we watched the exit of the supermarket I told Cody about Elizabeth's impromptu visit. He'd already heard the initial parts of it from Maya on the way over.

"Christ, we've been earning our pay on this one. You sound like you kept your cool, or is that a cleaned up version? I know Maya left to avoid blowing up at her."

"Not that much. Maya and I both reeled it in pretty well, I think. But Elizabeth is really over the edge. I can see why the family just lets her be off in her own exile without protesting."

"I'm glad that I'm not blessed with a writer's ability, you know?" he said. "Because people like her you could not invent, and you would almost have to. She has her own kind of reality that most of us never encounter."

"She must put your old psychology background in motion again."

"Give me a day with her and I could still do a complete diagnosis."

I wondered whether he could've stood an entire day with her. A dozen people emerged from the store in a group and we looked them over carefully.

"Still feeling good about Carlos?" I said after a while.

"As much as ever. He had all the tells. I've seen it a thousand times before. Innocent people don't run away after overturning a cast iron table on you. You know what the best tell for innocence is that I've ever seen?"

"What?"

"You make an appointment and the suspect shows up for an interrogation on time—you never have to go out and pick him up—and he doesn't think he needs a lawyer. Sometimes bringing legal counsel along doesn't even occur to him. Then he doesn't insist on telling you far more than you ask. He just answers all the questions that he can and he's even able to admit he doesn't know the answer to some of them."

"I can see that, but I wish we had some physical evidence too."

Cody rolled up his sleeve to show the elbow. His hand made a fist. "How about this? Wanna see the scars on my knees?"

"I guess you've earned your dollar here too."

Just after six o'clock Ximena Altamirano emerged from the supermarket exit no longer wearing the vest. Walking toward us without looking in our direction, she reached the corner of the building and continued along the façade facing the parking lot until she paused at a white Mercedes sedan waiting in the pregnant customer row. She climbed in.

"Damn!" Cody said. "We were so busy watching the exit for her that we didn't see him pull up. We could've busted him right here if you'd parked across his rear while I pointed my gun at his face through the window."

This was true. I wondered what it was going to take to reel him in now. At least they hadn't seen Cody, and like Ximena, Carlos had never met me. Pulling out of the lot, Cody kept another car between them and us. I hadn't been able to get a good look at the driver, but we were both certain it had to be Carlos in that car.

The white Mercedes left the parking lot and went around the *glorieta* in front of the old Real del Conde building and came back up past La Luciérnaga. The Libramiento, the ring road that circles most of San Miguel, was fairly busy at that hour, and it was not difficult to keep two or three cars between us. Neither of us had much to say. We were both considering what was coming next. The hardest part was going to be delivering

Carlos uninjured into the unenthusiastic hands of Diego Delgado. Our prey was not driving faster than the rest of the pack, so he was drawing no special attention except from us.

Were we acting like vigilantes in doing this? I suppose, but we had helped Delgado on a number of previous cases and he had helped us. We had a track record of acting as police backup several times, and our relationship had never been what anyone would call *formal*. Rules get bent, partial truths get told. Cases get solved, mostly. The relationship was elastic and usually effective, and that was all we could ask. And it worked.

At the bottom of the hill by La Comer, formerly the Mega supermarket, the Mercedes circled another *glorieta* and started up the Salida a Celaya, the Celaya highway. Did that mean they were staying out of town? That would make sense. There was less traffic there so we hung back a bit further. Half a kilometer up the slope they swerved into the right lane and slowed for the speed bumps.

"Looks like they're going into Los Faroles," Cody said.

If there was an early housing development in San Miguel, before all the other gated communities, that would be Los Faroles (The Lanterns). It was a large tract that sloped down toward the reservoir and the railroad tracks. From the architectural style, it suggested the early seventies. Like many developments that had set out to be consciously fashionable in their time (I don't say cutting edge), it now looked dated and left behind. Nearly half of the lots had never been built on, so the ambience also carried a note of unfulfilled optimism, and of running out of gas.

It was no surprise that house prices were quite reasonable there compared with many other neighborhoods closer in. Some houses were not occupied, and others were, but for only brief periods each year. Driving through, I always thought it lacked commitment. For me the color of the light there had always been a shade off and the sun seemed dimmer. It was rather sad. You could see that the place once had some momentum, but that was all history now, since the charm of its early years had mainly been novelty—that most fugitive of assets.

The white Mercedes pulled in and drove through the arched gateway. In the eighteen years I've lived in San Miguel I had never seen a gate or security guard there to screen visitors, although that must once have been the intent. Cody paused the Ford in the shadow of the archway. When Carlos and Ximena were about a hundred meters beyond, we followed them in.

One amenity the development offered was a group of welcoming public spaces. A series of small squares presented benches and fountains, although the neglected plantings had a tired and dusty look now. The

Mercedes turned left at the far corner of one of these empty gathering spots. We turned left at the near corner to keep Carlos in view. There was little other traffic.

A block further on stood a building everyone called the Clinic, although originally it must've had a different name. Built in a more traditional style than most of Los Faroles, it had once been a plastic surgery facility designed to look like a two-story house in a residential neighborhood. It was a discreet retreat to be reconstructed in at favorable prices. Americans and Canadians must've streamed in during its heyday. I wasn't aware of any other businesses now operating there, and this one had been closed for many years. The building had been offered for sale intermittently, but so much remodeling would've been required to turn it into a livable house that with so many other listings, the neighborhood didn't appear to justify the investment. Now the dark blood-red paint was blotchy and peeling with water spots. That said something about the roof. As we surveyed it from a distance, the Mercedes stopped before the garage door and Carlos got out to lift it open. We were hiding behind a tall and bushy pair of agave in the tiny local plaza.

"That is definitely him, so that computes, doesn't it," Cody said. "Who's going to bother them in there?"

"We are. I'm glad he didn't abandon the car somewhere else because that'll be our rationale for taking him down. Two public-spirited expat citizens spot a stolen Mercedes Benz on the street. You never know. Delgado will question him, and Carlos will assume it's about the murder. He might make some mistakes that he can't recover from." We were still a dozen men in Kevlar vests short of a swat team, so the question of how to bring him out was now the main issue. "One of us could ring the doorbell as a Fuller Brush man."

Cody wiped this aside. "No disguises this time, OK? Nothing off the shelf ever fits me here."

We waited in the car for a while but neither of us thought they were coming out again. After all, Ximena worked at the supermarket. If they had needed something for dinner she would've brought it with her. The check out girls shared tips with the packers.

"We're going in," Cody said. Now he sounded like some kind of squad leader.

"Sounds good, but how? Did you ever notice how all the cops here have bulletproof vests and helmets? Why is that? You're a bigger target than I am. Give it some thought."

"Carlos is unlikely to be armed," Cody said. "He doesn't have the money to even pick up a dirty street gun for five hundred pesos ($26 US) at the Tuesday Market. We've got them cornered."

I thought this might be optimistic. "Right, but how do we get in?" Aside from the garage door, there was only a small street door at the corner. In the absence of any windows facing the street we got out and walked around it. It was a steel door with three rows of round studs, an iron ring for a door handle, and at eye level, a small door about four by eight inches. This was what I called a face door. "So this won't work," I said. "Since Carlos raised the garage door by hand, I'm guessing there's no electricity inside, and he can probably lock it after he comes in. After all, no one has lived there in a generation. If we try to do the same thing it'll make a lot of noise without getting us in. If we go pound on the entry, the tiny door at eye level opens and immediately slams shut again. Game over, man."

"But these will get us in quietly enough." Cody pulled a small leather case off his belt; his lock picks.

"You're not at all queasy about breaking and entering, are you?" I said, pulling out my gun.

He gave me a blank look. "We've done it before, Paul. How else are we going to get at him?"

"We could wait until he comes out to take Ximena to work in the morning."

"And what time would that be?"

"Maybe eight o'clock."

"Then we'll probably have a car chase through morning rush hour traffic with her in the passenger seat. And you know they won't be wearing seat belts. How much sense does that make?"

"You'd rather break the law," I said.

He shrugged. "It's a lawless land, and I'm not talking about the drug trade. Did you ever see anyone stop for a stop sign here?"

"Only to avoid a fatal accident."

"Then we're going in."

"Hold on a second." I pulled out my cell and dialed Delgado. When he picked up we went through the usual greetings.

"How can I help you today, Señor Zacher, at a time when you are working so late as this?"

"We have located Carlos Fuentes, the driver in the Cavaletti murder case. You have an outstanding charge of auto theft on him for that missing Mercedes."

"Yes, well that is good news indeed." Nothing more. Not even, Where is he?

"He is inside the old Clinic building in Los Faroles."

"OK, thank you so much for this information. I am making a note of it now."

More silence. "Do you plan to pick him up?"

"Well, as you will understand, the evening crew has just come on and we are slightly shorthanded. Perhaps in the morning we will find a better opportunity."

I wished him luck and signed off. Perhaps I shouldn't have been surprised. "Go ahead with those picks," I said to Cody. "Nobody's coming to pick him up."

CHAPTER NINETEEN

Cody bent over the lock and went to work. It wasn't that I was afraid of a confrontation; my principle fear was that we might kill either or both of them. If Carlos was guilty, then he was going to throw everything he could think of at us. Ximena might try to protect him, or step in front of him, or just take a ricocheting bullet. This could turn into a real mess, but I couldn't think of any other way to free Miss Rachel. It was clear that Mark Savio and his local support team hadn't either, and he was making in an hour what I was making in a day.

"This is a very nasty little beast," Cody muttered through his teeth after four or five minutes. "It's the worst one I've tried to pick down here so far, even worse than that one in Chiapas. Five or ten years of disuse is not a good start for this project. I wish I had some lubricant to spray in there." Then he got into a gentle up and down massage of the tumblers inside. I kept watching for traffic, but on the side streets of Los Faroles nothing was moving. If a person's primary goal was a quiet lifestyle, undisturbed by the tourists and the holiday fireworks, this was the place to live.

Cody switched picks, swore quietly after a brief struggle with the new one, and then switched back again. Even though this was an intensely subtle operation, the sweat was breaking out on his forehead. Another five minutes passed with mounting frustration. Fortunately, this process made little noise. Carlos would not have heard us from inside unless his ear was directly against the lock on the other side.

"Is there anything I can do to help?" I said softly.

"Yes, keep quiet and watch the street. Don't talk to me." His tone was crisper than usual.

I took a step back to avoid casting a shadow on his labors. From a block and a half away I glimpsed a woman walking a white yappy shorthaired dog on a leash. I wasn't sure if she could see us or not. We were on the shady side of the Clinic and she was in the sun, now starting to make longer shadows that reached across the street toward her path. I looked at my watch. It was 6:35. When I glanced back in her direction, she and the dog were gone. I was relieved. A lot of dogs have too canny a sense for intruders for the comfort of anyone who is one. Stealth was not my usual style, but when you're acting that way, you can feel like there's a spotlight on your every move. Cody grunted softly and slid the pick out of the lock. Lifting on the handle to prevent a squeak of the hinges, no better maintained than the lock, I'm sure, he pushed the door slowly open into a shadowy corridor. We slipped inside, leaving it open.

Naturally Cody and I found no lingering smell of death or anesthetic in that corridor, and I'm not sure why I expected one. Maybe I associated hospitals of any kind with bad news. To me they meant death or bank-ruptcy or often both. But this clinic had been for plastic surgery. No one would've died there, hopefully. Nor did we hear any sound inside. That probably meant no one had heard us coming in either. Cody now had his gun out too.

A long time had passed since I had been inside this clinic, although it was not to have my eyebrows re-shaped or my butt recontoured. It was during the time before I bought my house on Quebrada, and I needed an empty place with flexible spaces where I could carve out a studio besides the normal living quarters. The Clinic had provided too many of them, but none of them had good natural light. Adequate surgical light comes from the electric company, not the sun.

We paused to get a sense of the layout. My rec-ollection of the interior was sketchy, other than that it possessed what by now was a period operating room. I must've found it as charmless and lacking potential then as I did now. The corridor stopped at the far end with a staircase on the left and an exit to the garden on the right. Imagine a footprint like a bracket with one long side, capped by two short ends pointing in the same direction. Running parallel to the long side between the short sides was a narrow garden courtyard where nothing remained alive, although the trunks of two dead trees remained upright. All the windows on the corridor faced this barren open space, which was bordered by a blank two-story wall on the opposite side, where large amorphous chunks of unpainted plaster had fallen to the ground to reveal crude red brick beneath.

The ambient light from the cloudy windows was chancy but still functional. As this encounter played out we would be losing more of it by the minute.

"They must be upstairs," Cody whispered.

"As I recall, quite vaguely, there are living quarters up there next to an open rooftop terrace. I don't remember the layout any better than that."

"OK, how about this. I'll go up the steps and flush him out. In the meantime you're checking this row of rooms, whatever they are, and if he gets past me and comes down the steps, you will take him down without shooting him. He'll either be going for the garage and out that way, or back the way we just came in."

"And if he's already in those rooms?"

"I don't think he will be, but if he has a round cast iron table with him, keep a little distance between the two of you, OK?"

Cody marched silently down the corridor ahead of me, glancing into the rooms as he went by. I decided to take a more detailed look once he reached the stairs and started on his way up. Overhead the paint was curling off the ceiling and flaking onto the floor.

The first door was locked. It bore a small tablet of a metal sign that read, Farmacia. Watch those expiration dates, I thought. Even the aspirin will go bad sooner or later. Three rooms followed that had been patient spaces. The beds were still there, each with a dirty mattress but no linens, and a small bathroom alcove in one corner. This was followed by an open space with a center island, probably the nurses' station. There was a door on the back wall that must've led into the garage. The debris on the floor leading to it was disturbed along a pathway from the corridor as if by footprints. The fixtures were covered by flaked paint and dust. So far, nothing was moving and I heard no sound from upstairs.

Then a woman's voice tore through the silence. It must've been Ximena, although I had only heard her speak once before in a low tone to greet me at the supermarket check out counter. I could only make out her tone, not her words, so I stayed in the shadows near the nurses' station, listening. A moment later, at the sound of running footsteps approaching, I poised myself for a leap once Carlos got close, wishing now that we hadn't left the outside door open. He would never take the time to go through the garage, pull the door open, and start the car if anyone was close on his heels.

Jamming my gun in my belt, I leaped into the corridor, prematurely, as it happened, because all I saw in response was a sprinting figure that turned abruptly into the next room. It had a pair of swinging doors for an entry, and both were standing open. I moved silently up the hallway. The doors gave access through the corner of the room, so that the longer part of it stretched away to the right and was in deep shadow. Listening intently, and seeing no sign of Carlos, I pulled out my gun again, wondering where Cody was at that moment.

I began to slide along the wall, facing the room. In the center was an operating table on a heavy iron base. It had a wheel on the thick tapered cylindrical shaft to raise or lower it. Overhead a semi-spherical lamp hung on an adjustable bracket. Against the wall at the left were two rolling gurneys. The wall opposite had rows of shelving covered by floor to ceiling doors, some hanging open, some not. The depth of the room on the right was too obscure to make out the detail. I continued to creep along the wall, my gun extended, wishing for a flashlight to rake the interior. Then I stopped as I heard the minutest of noises at the far end, the darkest part.

At my shoulder an open shelf unit protruded from the wall about eighteen inches and I stepped out to clear it. The shelves were thick with powdery debris under my hand. The fine hairs on my neck stood up. As I wiped my hand on my pants I heard the sound of wheels on the concrete floor, starting up very fast. I began to turn around toward the entry but at that moment something hit me in the lower back and I flew forward onto my face. The gun spun away out of my raised hand, skittering out of sight.

Immediately I swung around to get on my back, the pain running down both my legs. Carlos leaped toward me, his hand coming up. I raised both legs and caught him in the chest, thrusting him backward, but a searing pain tore a path down my thigh.

The impact of my heels thrust him over and he fell sideways. I heard a knife or scalpel slide past me on the concrete. Then Carlos was on his feet. I struggled to get up.

"Paul! Paul! Where are you?" Cody's voice echoed the length of the corridor.

"In surgery!" I felt this was true in several ways.

Carlos was already running toward the exit by the time Cody arrived. He may even have been through it by then. I was standing up, a little shaky, gripping the shelf unit. The pain in my lower back had me bending over slightly. Blood was running down my left leg into my shoe.

"I'm OK, go after him!"

Cody wheeled out of the room, but I didn't think he'd be able to catch up with Carlos. I staggered out into the hallway. Outside, through the open door we'd come through, a swirl of red and blue lights swept the street beyond. I had never seen anything so welcome as I hobbled down the hall.

Outside in the twilight Officer Hugo Peña and one other I didn't recognize had Carlos handcuffed and were loading him into the back seat of a police pickup. He didn't appear to be injured. Diego Delgado was talking to Cody. I saw no special excitement in his manner. In the past I had noticed that he often seemed calmer after the fight was over than I was. My pounding pulse said I was still winding down. I borrowed a flashlight from him and went back inside after my gun.

In the operating room with that focused light I first found my own blood on the grubby floor, a long smear with a lot of scattered droplets. I scanned the foot-long slash through my pants leg. My thigh would probably need some disinfectant. The blood flow was slowing now, although I saw it had stained my hands and was smeared on the flashlight too. After a painful search where I was mostly on the floor rubbing my back with one hand, I found my gun under the four-footed iron base of an old-fashioned scale, the kind you would stand on while the nurse slid the weights around until they balanced.

When I came outside again, the pickup with Carlos was gone. Cody and Delgado were laughing. I hung back for a while; any laugh would've caused me a lot of pain. No more blood was flowing out of my pants, and I could feel the long scalpel cut like a burn running down the front of my thigh. Even if my leg and back didn't, I still felt good in a more general way. It was over and it could've been much worse, not just for us, but for everyone. I was pleased to note that they had not dragged Ximena downstairs for this. She had gone through far more than she deserved. For a criminal apprehension, it met Maya's highest criterion: no one had died, or even been badly injured. I pulled out my phone and told her exactly that.

"Well, Señor Zacher," Delgado said, placing his hand on my shoulder, "you have done yourself some credit on this evening, and now you bear the injuries of the honorable and the just."

This was more credit than I usually got, even from Maya.

"Thank you, but it wouldn't have ended in this way if you hadn't come when you did."

"Well, as for that, I had some second thoughts after I spoke with you today. Why not, as I said to myself, to give some backup to these very serious people? Right or wrong I don't know, but they have backed me up a number of times in the past. Do you know this?"

"I do now, and thank you again."

"Can you find your own medical assistance, or should I call for you the Cruz Roja?"

"Thank you. I'll be OK if I can just clean up the blood a little. We'll take Cody's car."

He called to one of the remaining officers, who brought a large plastic evidence bag to cover my leg in the car. The shoes, a seven-year-old pair of Ecco trainers I had bought on a long shopping weekend in Laredo, would now have their final days expensed to Miss Rachel, as well as my jeans. The injuries to my thigh were no more than wear and tear, as it often comes from life.

Before we drove off, I said to Delgado, "Please do not charge anything against Carlos for my injuries, because I will not sign a *denuncia* (complaint). We were acting informally, as you know. If he is guilty of killing Señor Cavaletti, that's all we need to know to close out this case."

Through Cody's open passenger side window, he prudently waved instead of shaking my bloody hand as we pulled away.

CHAPTER TWENTY
LUC CAVALETTI

That evening Luc Cavaletti waited in the great room, and hearing the door close on the lower level, intercepted his brother Rocco as he came bounding up the main staircase two steps at a time. He had been out running on the narrow street that fronted the property, and from there, twice around Parque Juarez below, yet he still had the energy to sprint up two flights of steps inside. Luc shook his head. At thirty he was starting to develop a modest yet comfortable bulge over his belt. He had started buying new silk shirts he didn't have to tuck into his pants.

He waved to his brother. "I want to talk to you about something, Rocco. We've got some problems in the company. Why not have a glass of wine with me on the terrace?"

"Sure, but I'm kind of sweaty." Rocco shrugged and made a half humorous gesture as if to sniff his shirt in disgust.

"Don't worry about it. Tonight it's only going to be the two of us. I've already opened a bottle out there. It's the '04 Gran Reserva."

It was at the time of evening that was neither dark nor light. They had no knowledge of Paul Zacher, Diego Delgado, and the drama below at the other end of the city. A tentative and exhausted finish had settled along the horizon, one that reflected the uncertainty of the past fifteen days. At the rim of darkness a reddish sun struggled to make a farewell statement among the trailing shredded clouds. The breeze had recently fallen away and the palm trees edging the terrace were at rest. Beneath their branches the shadows were already thick and opaque. It felt like the relief of having another frustrating day gone, coupled with the uncertainty of what tomorrow might bring for the Cavaletti family. Still, this was only the mood set by the weather. Luc tried without success to recall the last upbeat day they had experienced. Earlier, they had always been so much the norm that he never noticed them as such.

By this time Mark Savio had already brought Luc and Rocco up to date on the provisions of their father's will, and since Miss Rachel was now both the interim heir as trustee for both of them, and the primary suspect in Sebastian's murder, the situation was worse than merely equivocal. During her absence in jail, now quite possibly developing into a long one, they were faced with running the vineyard without the authority to make any important decisions. In this pre-trial period they could only communicate with her through her attorney. Privately, Luc thought Mark Savio was a self-important buffoon. He may have, as he bragged, clerked for a time in Melvin Belli's office. He may also have been a star in San Francisco legal circles, but he had little chance of getting anything accomplished in San Miguel. Luc believed Miss Rachel may have seen her attorney as a long unfulfilled romantic fantasy. That was an idea he found revolting.

Less than three feet apart across a small wicker lamp table, the brothers sat down on the broad terrace, with the great room fireplace chimney at their backs, and surveyed the finishing moves of the day. The darkening sky had the character of a grand but fugitive painting taking shape, only to be forever lost a few moments later. During the day the clouds had appeared bright and dynamic, but now they suggested nothing but gathering thunder. Luc refreshed his own glass and poured out a new one for his brother.

"Here's to surviving in tough times," said Rocco, raising his wineglass. With a sigh he stretched out his legs and rested his heels on a wicker hassock. He flexed his calf muscles as he looked out of the corner of his eye at his brother.

From the sconce lights at the doorway, Luc saw the hint of discomfort in his face, mainly in his jaw, his lips, and in his eyes, which appeared crimped and tense as if he was squinting at something threatening in the future. "We've had many better. There were times in the past when we were up and down, and you've seen how that goes, but they were never as bad as this. We can feel the whole thing falling in on us now, and with too many limitations on how we can respond."

Luc took a thoughtful sip of the elegant wine. At least there was always that kind of consolation in his glass, even when there were few others. The family business, and his role in it, had always been the focus of this life, and if women had never provided a serious distraction for him as they did for his father, they would even less so now in this crisis. Part of what he was looking for was an idea of what to expect from Rocco as this deteriorated further. He already had some ideas about that. In his business life Luc was used to reading trend lines, and he couldn't see this one improving much. The main theme that lately came to mind was *damage control*, and that didn't only refer to public relations. Beyond this, he and his brother had never talked privately about their father's passing. That was not unusual; they had never been close. With a difference of three years in their ages, it always seemed to Luc that Rocco had rejected any idea of competing with him. He would've welcomed it if he'd tried. It could've meant the combining of forces in a situation like this.

"I don't know what more we can do from here," Rocco said. "At least at home, we could keep things going."

"Proactive is what I always do at home. We can do it from here too."

"But what does that mean in this place? We don't even have the language to do business."

Luc turned more toward his brother and crossed his legs. "Let me start by saying that I don't trust Paul Zacher. It's not that he's a bad person, but he works for Miss Rachel. And worse, I don't trust that Delgado guy with the police, either. He's got his own agenda." Zacher had seemed subtly aloof when they talked. Luc had come away with the sense that the detective didn't think him up to the task of taking over the vineyard. As if his main job of waiting in the wings had never taught him anything. He had always been, in fact, a careful observer.

"So who are you going to trust?" Rocco said. "You said you thought Mark Savio is a fool."

Luc nodded slowly. "I still do. You won't believe this, but here it is as a remedy for tough times. I would like to trust *us*. There's an important role here for both of us." Luc watched his brother's reaction carefully.

Rocco shrugged and turned away. "Wow! Trust is a big word for having only five letters. Sometimes I don't even trust Rathbone."

This was not the reply Luc expected. "You can

trust him to keep his mouth shut, at least. But for me, the word us does not include him or Celeste or our mother. I'm talking about you and me, the remaining family that's still capable of doing anything. Mom has always been out of it and this is not going to bring her back in."

"And you don't think Miss Rachel killed Dad? Is that what you're saying?"

"No, I don't. Not a chance." Luc drained his glass with the feeling that he was not paying enough attention to the subtlety of the wine, and poured another round. That finished the bottle, but another one waited below on the shelf of the wicker table at his side. After all, wine was meant to be drunk, and any occasion could be improved by the right bottle.

"So then there's the driver, Carlos," Rocco said. "Zacher thinks he did it because Dad was messing around with that girl from the kitchen. I guess they were a couple until that happened. Miss Rachel told me about that."

Luc was a long time in answering. "Perhaps. Perhaps not."

"You don't think Dad was all over that little *chica*?"

"No, I'm sure he was. That's exactly the kind of thing he would do. You must've noticed her. I'm just not sure that Carlos was the one that killed him because of it."

"You think the girl could've done it herself?" Rocco said.

Luc nearly chuckled. "I doubt she had it in her to kill him. Dad's death may have been about a woman, that would surprise no one in this family, and it would be fitting in a twisted way, but probably not that particular woman, not an appealing young kitchen girl who didn't feel she had the social status to resist him. In this country I'm sure dozens of men have handled her a little as they came on to her before. She has to be used to it."

"So, not that one." Rocco's voice, which could sometimes be harsh and blunt, had become quieter than the night now falling with gradual finality below the rim of the terrace. Like a single thread of desperate lightning, a ragged line of reddish orange edged parts of the choppy profile of the San Miguel skyline far beyond.

"You seem to know something, Luc, or at least, you think you know something," Rocco added, guiding his empty glass closer to his brother, who reached onto the lower shelf of the table and brought up the other bottle of the Gran Reserva. He pulled a waiting corkscrew from his pants pocket and cut the foil at the neck with a single gesture.

"These things can be very complicated," Luc said, stripping the foil from the neck of the bottle. It fell unnoticed to the floor. With another practiced stroke he extracted the cork with a modest pop, sniffed it, and handed it to Rocco. "Orchids and young apricots, with a hint of toasted almonds and a note of black raspberry.

As always, this is a bottle that is more about complete satisfaction than surprise. That year of 2004 has always been the essence of consistency, all across the property." He refilled their glasses, thinking how easy it was to fall back into his normal vineyard role. That would still pay off in the future, once all this was past them. Luc didn't care for contingencies like that.

"God knows we could also use some consistency in our lives in other areas," said Rocco, taking a long sip of the wine. He found it exactly the same as always: authoritative, robust, and yet full of subtlety at the same time. He hesitated to admit this to his brother.

Luc slipped the corkscrew back in his pocket. "Dad was always consistent, but where did that get him? Now he's dead before his sixtieth birthday. Men in his position should be able to go on and on until they can't walk anymore or even think straight, don't you think?"

"Yes," Rocco said, "and until they can't screw anybody anymore either. And then you would take over. You've always been waiting in the wings for this moment. Too bad Miss Rachel got the big prize, though. That must be hard to swallow."

Luc sat there in silence, startled for a moment. "Then maybe it should've been you? Is that what you're saying? Just how would that work? You're always out running, blowing off steam, but you never seem to generate any for the business. A company like this is all about momentum, market share, and image, aside from the grapes, the season, and the winemaker." This was a conversation that had often seemed to hang in the air between them, but they had rarely touched on it in the past. Rocco gave an ironic laugh and shook his head. "No, Bro, I would never suggest anything like that. I guess I know my role in this family only too well, and I always have. I'm the misfit, the one that didn't work out as everybody hoped. The one they buy off on the payroll every month. Don't worry at all about that. No one understands better than I do why I could never take Dad's place, even if I'd ever wanted to try. I could never find the key. I was born with the right credentials but I could never make them work."

Luc had long shared this thought too. An ugly conclusion came to him, and not for the first time. What did Rocco's last sentence mean? This was the moment. He took a while to frame his next question with precision as he refilled their glasses. In the dim light his smile was less innocent than he tried to make it.

"I want to let you in on something, Rocco. You may not want to hear it. Celeste came on to me at home a week or so before we came down here. She said she would do me any way I wanted it, even some I had never thought of. Naturally I brushed her off, but that made me stop and wonder what else might be going on that I didn't know about. My only thought was that she was still with Dad. I had no reason to compete with him for her attention. What do you suppose she was thinking?"

Rocco stared at him blankly for a long moment before he spoke. "Of course, she would always be with Dad as long as he lived. That was a given, even if it wasn't always what she wanted to do most."

As darkness settled over the terrace, Luc switched on the ceramic lamp between them. Under its parchment shade it was meant to be more intimate than bright, but still Rocco turned his face toward the darkness beyond the terrace. His phrase, "as long as he lived," stayed in Luc's mind.

"Later I began to wonder whether you did have a reason to compete with Dad," Luc continued, "because if Celeste made that offer to me, then why not to you? What if she was working her way through the men around her to see what response she could turn up? A trim buff guy like the younger son, a family insider not quite at the top but still hungry, so why would she not hedge her bets? Celeste is an experienced climber, I saw that from the beginning in the way she got her hooks into Dad in no time."

Although an uneasy smile had settled on Rocco's features, he didn't reply, so Luc went on.

"Then why isn't she now screwing Paul Zacher's brains out, for example? A guy who could definitely have some influence on the way this goes, since he's connected with the police here. I'm telling you I would not be surprised at all. Why would he keep her at arm's length? I have no idea. Yes, his Mexican girlfriend is a hottie, but how long is it since he's been with a real blonde? As Celeste would be so quick to remind him."

Luc did not regret now finding himself throwing mud scooped from this particular gutter. He preferred being high minded, but it didn't always win the case. All his life he had struggled to accept Rocco, but he had never really been able to. The kid might have been an alien that had been planted in his mother's womb by some night creature, a foreigner. Rocco had always lacked the innate strength of character that had raised the Cavaletti family from nickel and dime jug wines to rank among the top Sonoma County growers in just two generations. Luc firmly believed that leadership talent was all in the genes, just as it was with the grapes. Breeding was the issue, and that didn't mean sleeping with some cheap climber just because she called your name in a seductive tone.

Rocco's blunted expression told Luc he had scored by bringing in Paul Zacher's name. The younger brother looked morosely through his glass toward the long darkened cityscape, now speckled with hopeful lights, but found only a void confirmed beyond. Finally he spoke.

"Maybe you'd like to think you were the only one she wanted, as the obvious heir to the throne. That she would go wild over you and kick people like me aside as everybody else does. And by the way, by the fucking way, Celeste would never screw some local zero like Paul Zacher. She has some class. Maybe a lot more than you think, maybe even more than you have, Bro, king of the local fucking mountain wherever you go and spread your business card around as people lick your shoes. Here's the irony: you don't even know who you really are." Rocco's voice trailed off inaudibly on the last sentence and Luc missed its meaning. Rocco often ended his statements in a mutter, as if he didn't expect anyone to listen.

An extended silence settled over them. Perhaps this conversation had been a long time coming and left both of them in need of catching their breath. Luc found himself following the dots, since the clues were all there. Earlier, he had not thought this possible, but he was still ready to try. He was nodding as he spoke. "How did Dad find out about you and Celeste? Did he catch you in bed with her? Was she probing your sore spots after a long run?"

A queasy grin came over Rocco's face. Luc had seen it before. It was the same look he'd displayed every time he'd been caught misbehaving as a child. Some things never change, Luc thought. But something had changed here, in the last fifteen days. Sebastian Cavaletti, the patriarch, was dead. The damp patches beneath Rocco's arms on the neon shirt were spreading larger than they'd been when he returned from running. He began to shake his head.

"Dad just guessed. You know how he could read some people in a heartbeat. Well, he read me, I suppose. Maybe it was in my face or my attitude; I don't know."

"What did he say to you?"

"He said he would kick me out of the family for messing around with her. That I must've forced her into it. He said I had drawn my last paycheck from the company and he was going to write me out of the will too. When we got home, I could clear my stuff out of the house immediately. I was on my own."

"That was harsh." Shaking his head, Luc could imagine this scene perfectly.

"I was shocked. I had never been on my own before, and it was a new idea. We were out here on the terrace. He was sitting where you are now. Then he just stood up and went back into the great room. I could see how worked up he was. That guitar music inside became louder, as if he was trying to shut some thoughts out of his head."

"And you came in after him."

"Yes, but at first I was scared, and I was going to apologize. I had always known I had gone too far. He was standing at the top of the steps, his shoulders hunched over, his fists clenched at first, then gripping his shoulders, and the rage was coming off him in waves. I know you've seen him like that before. Suddenly the sight of him like that made me so angry too that I couldn't stand it. All the shit I've taken from this family just came up in a big pile in front of me. Somehow for the first time in my life, I couldn't jump over it but I knew I could run around it, OK? I thought I was better than somebody else. That came from the way Celeste screamed when I screwed her."

Luc was nodding now. He could see it so well, although Cindy, his own wife, had not screamed in a long time. "So instead of apologizing, you grabbed the poker and hit him with it."

"No, it was the cane, Miss Rachel's heavy cane right there on the end of the sofa. I didn't even slow down coming in. My hand just found it, my fingers closed around it as if it was meant to be. I never even understood what I was doing until Dad stopped at the bottom of the stairs in a pile. He never uttered a sound."

"And I'm sure you felt sickened at what you had done."

"No. I felt surprised that it actually happened like that. I ran down the steps to see if he was still alive, but he looked dead right away. I took the elevator back up and went to my room."

"And you could go to sleep after that?"

"No! I read my weightlifting magazine until Rathbone woke up the house about half an hour later. I couldn't tell you now what article I was reading. I don't think I really saw a single word of it. All I could see was Dad's body in a pile." A long pause followed as if Rocco were reliving it. "I suppose you had figured all of this out already."

"I did have an inkling of it. I thought it was either you or the driver. Does Celeste know?"

Rocco nodded slowly. "I told her almost right away. I couldn't hold it back. She was really angry, but I had already done her. What happens now?"

"I'm not going to turn you in. But you have to realize that we're now in a very difficult position with regard to the vineyard. With Dad gone the only person in the company who can sign big checks is in jail down here. We can't even communicate with her directly. Try that for starters. And there are about fifty other things just as bad. We're frozen in place and every day it gets worse. I think you have to step forward and tell the police what happened. That's the only way we can get Miss Rachel released so she can take control again and do her job. Maybe you can get a plea deal for a charge of third degree homicide, whatever they call that here. The company will pay Savio to manage your defense."

"You must be kidding."

"Right now you are still in the will. You'll be able to inherit what you would've gotten, since Miss Rachel is the first heir in the chain, and you don't benefit directly from Dad's death. If you turn yourself in, I'll see that nothing changes in that regard. Otherwise I'll go to court back home and get it overturned."

When Rocco said nothing, Luc added, "But you have to do the right thing, and by that I mean be accountable for this. It will look better if you do it under your own power. If you think about it you'll see that it's in your interest too, since you're still a shareholder in the company. This is your chance to find out what you're made of, and I'm not going to make that call for you."

CHAPTER TWENTY-ONE

The call from Luc came in on my cell at about 8:30 in the morning. I'm an early riser most of the time and by then Maya and I were both finished with breakfast. His voice sounded loud enough but his tone was remote. That may have been a function of his mood more than his phone or something about the thick walls of the mansion. It also contained a hint of command, as if he was getting comfortable in his new role as interim chief operating officer of Cavaletti Vineyards.

"You need to have a conversation with Rocco this morning," Luc said. "It's important and it has a direct bearing on Miss Rachel's incarceration. I've told Rathbone to expect your arrival. He'll let you in and he can take you up to Rocco's room."

"Can you give me an idea what this is about?"

"I'm sorry that I won't be able to be there when you arrive." He hung up without adding any more.

"I heard most of that," Maya said with a frown.

"What do you think?"

"I don't like it and I think we ought to bring our guns."

We pulled them out of the bottom drawer inside the armoire, loaded them, checked them over, and left. It was not yet 8:45.

At nine o'clock we drove through the gates. We had not taken time to change into anything much more professional than our normal jeans and the loose cotton shirts we had pulled on to cover the guns on our hips. Maya had drawn her hair back into a ponytail, her action mode.

We drove out into a clear, crisp morning that promised some warmth later in the day. The sky was a featureless flat deep blue over the mansion, which loomed like a fortress from an earlier time. It did not seem to belong to San Miguel or to anywhere. It was now an oasis of wealth and pain. At that time of day all was profoundly silent. There was no activity around the parking area and I saw no movement in the windows. Rathbone met us at the door before we could press the button to ring for him.

He looked at Maya as if surprised to see her with me, but offered nothing except his conventional greeting. I almost told him she was the head of the Zacher Agency, but I held back, thinking we didn't need to explain anything to him. He was accustomed to functioning without explanations. We walked up the long flight of stairs. Un-expectedly they now had a runner in a muted Persian pattern that covered eight feet or so of the center from bottom to top. It made perfect sense, even if it had come a little too late to save Sebastian Cavaletti.

On the main floor Rathbone led us past the bar out onto the rectangle that framed the courtyard garden far below. We walked the length of one side and paused outside the first room in the corner.

"This is Rocco's bedroom." He turned and went back into the house.

"Are you feeling anything hinky about this?" Maya said, as we stood there for a moment watching Rathbone disappear.

"Everything has been hinky so far. I thought Elizabeth was hinky yesterday. Why would this be any different?"

I knocked twice on Rocco's door, and when there was no response, I turned the knob. It was not locked. The room was laid out on the same plan as his father's room, the one where I had met Celeste for the second time on Sebastian's bed. This bed was similar, but with a different headboard. It had once been made up, and the coverlet was now rumpled, but it didn't appear to have been turned down and slept in. On the bedside table was an empty bottle of the Cavaletti Gran Reserva next to a water glass bearing wine stains, now dry. Next to them were a wallet and a pair of keys on a tiny ring. The lamps on both nightstands were lit, although the sun had come up more than two hours before.

"I don't like this," Maya whispered. "Shouldn't he be here?"

A cold, dull feeling was coming over me. I didn't recognize it at first, but I should've. Looking back at that morning now, I think I didn't want to anticipate what was coming.

"He must be in the bathroom," I said, still taking a detailed inventory of the bedroom. Aside from a faintly stale odor, nothing seemed unusual. A slight glitter of light from the floor near the headboard caught my eye and I bent over to pick up a silver chain with a small amber heart in a silver bezel. The chain was broken, but it looked identical to the one I had seen on Celeste's neck when I visited her in Sebastian's bedroom.

Maya took it out of my hand and examined it.

"I think that belongs to Celeste," I said. She gave me a sharp look, then studied the bed.

"This must've been where Rocco and Celeste met," she said, "perhaps on some occasion when Sebastian had been called away. It might have been spur of the moment."

We were both shaking our heads as if we knew that wasn't true.

"Maybe the father was out again inspecting that

property on the Querétaro Road?" I said. "Maybe it only happened once." My impression of both Rocco and Celeste had shifted radically.

Had he been visiting other vineyards as a courtesy, or as a way of seeing how they operated with this climate and soil? As I stared at the bed, I still had difficulty seeing Celeste and Rocco together that way. It was not a four-poster, but it had tall spiral carved posts at both the headboard and footboard. Was that where they had hung their clothes? Or had they simply ripped them off and tossed them over the side to the floor? Perhaps they'd broken the delicate silver chain in a fit of passion and not even noticed it was gone.

Maya dropped it in her shirt pocket, buttoned it, and touched my elbow as if she knew what I was thinking too.

"Rocco," I called out quietly, and then again, louder. There was no answer. If he was gone, why had he left the door unlocked and the lights on? I turned away from the bed and found my feet were like lead.

The door to the dressing room was open halfway. I pushed it open further. Some of the drawers in the cabinet wall were open and several shirts had been dropped haphazardly on the floor. The lights were all turned on. As I stared for a moment at the bathroom door beyond I felt a further slow chill move over my skin. It was open about six inches. Maya had hung back behind me.

I blinked and turned away from the bathroom door, only to catch sight of myself in the tall mirror mounted on the wall near the cabinets. My stance looked edgy and tentative, both hands spread slightly outward at my sides as if I was unsure of my balance. On my left side Maya was watching me with a look of discomfort.

"Rocco," I said more sharply. "Are you in there?"

Silence.

"I'm not going any further," she said. "Just tell me if he's there. Say yes or no when you go in." She had folded her hands together beneath her chin.

"I shouldn't have brought you."

After a moment I pushed the bathroom door open and stepped into the room. There was only one thing to look at. Rocco Cavaletti was lying in the bathtub. He was dressed in running shorts and the same neon green shirt he'd been wearing when I talked to him originally. Reddish water covered most of his body. The twin shaving lights at the sink cast the scene in a terrible clarity, but sharply split between light and shadow. "Yes, he's in here," I finally said, over my shoulder.

Because Rocco was still dressed, the scene looked both frivolous and sinister at the same time, as if it had been a practical joke gone terribly wrong. His bare knees were raised an inch or two out of the water because his feet rested against the faucet end, and sticking up above the surface directly beneath the tap were the tips of his expensive athletic shoes, now stained reddish pink and drying at the toes. His head and shoulders were also clear of the water, resting on the sloped back of the tub.

Rocco's mouth and eyes were still open as if he had died in midsentence speaking to someone standing where I was now. His wrists and hands were under the pastel-tinted water from just above the elbows down. Like a horrifying afterthought, laying on the edge of the tub at the wall was a bloody paring knife. That there was no proper place to put it after using it mirrored in a minuscule way the utter chaos of the scene. I didn't have to lift Rocco's wrists from the water to know they must be slashed.

"Are you all right, Paul?" came Maya's small voice from the dressing room.

"Yes, but Rocco is dead by his own." That was how she would've said it. "You don't have to come in if you don't want to see this. Don't worry, I didn't want to see this either."

I placed my palm on his cheek for a moment. It was cold and already too firm to the touch. I had no idea how long he'd been dead, but the scene with both the water and the body gone cold like that, probably to the same temperature, displayed an irreversible finality, as if it ended more than just his life. Why was he still dressed, even to his shoes? Had he not wished to add that further degree of pathetic victimhood that would've come with being naked and half submerged in the blood-tinted water? Yet, it was that same victimhood that he had embraced with a tone of self-righteousness when I spoke with him. Victimhood can be a life script, I thought.

"Are you still OK in there, Paul? Is there anything we can do for him?"

I think of OK as describing a condition of easy equilibrium with reality, and that was far out of my reach in that moment. It was only then I noticed a note resting on the lid of the toilet. A sheet of typing paper with two lines of words scrawled irregularly over it in a black felt tip pen. It looked as if it had been written in a car moving over rough pavement or cobblestones. It appeared that Rocco Cavaletti had been in a hurry at the end, having made up his mind to kill himself at a point when he was none too steady, and he didn't want to entertain any second thoughts.

I killed the old man now I'll see him again.

For Rocco, did the afterlife signify a place where murderer and victim would be reunited to compare notes or patch things up again? I didn't touch the paper, trying to imagine the logic behind this, although the scene around me displayed little logic of any kind. Was this about Celeste? I could only speculate. How many different ways did she relate to men? When she was flirting with me I assumed it was mainly because she was looking for a new career position. But what if that was her everyday manner, even before Sebastian's death?

Perhaps she was a buccaneer, a player in the same way Sebastian had been, and he had caught them together.

I don't read much fiction except for some of the British writers, like Graham Greene, but one plot line I always enjoy is about the guy who falls for a woman who is wrong for him in every way, and the subsequent damage it does to his life, and often, to hers. Even though I hadn't always made choices as good as Maya, this did not reflect my own course through life. I don't think I'm capable of making a complete fool of myself in that way. Still, that scenario fascinates me for reasons I can't explain. As I stood there in the bathroom, the scene of Rocco's final moments, I wondered if this realization had come to him too—that he had made a colossal and irreversible mistake. In some ways, suicide might not be that different from more normal ways of dying, ones you could see approaching in the distance; you still had to come to terms with it, to take it by the hand.

I looked into Rocco's cold and silent face again. I could not have said I found any real expression around the slack appearance of his open mouth, but his final look was not one of sadness. More than that I couldn't have characterized it. When he lowered his slashed wrists into the warm water and watched his life swirl around him as it flowed away, had he reviewed the progression of events that culminated in that moment? Was Celeste's face the last thing he saw, or was it that of his father, beckoning to him from the other side?

At the same time, I suppose it was a triumph of sorts for Rocco, since he had done something very powerful on this visit to México, probably for the first time in his life. He had made a statement that could neither be contradicted nor ignored.

I turned and walked back into the dressing room, closing the bathroom door after me.

Here was the choice Maya and I faced. We could call the police and have the house sealed yet again, or we could call our doctor, who would come and give a death certificate with much less fuss or inconvenience to the residents. Given the history of the case, with Miss Rachel still locked up, and the circumstances of the body, I called Delgado and had to leave a message. We went back into the bedroom. I studied the scene again, and as I waited for him to return the call I could not help but realize that Rocco's act of making a statement that could neither be contradicted nor ignored was also my own goal every time I picked up a paintbrush. If art is different from life, is it also that different from death? We could take this up in the final case report where I would have a little more mental space for speculation. That was always my time to try to make sense of a case, even if it was mostly for myself.

"How ugly was it?" Maya said after a while, her arms folded.

"It's always ugly. He cut his wrists in the tub."

"You're sure he's dead?"

"Yes, he's dead. It must've happened last night because the body is quite cold."

Her lips tightened and she nodded.

"Take a look if you want. I'll wait right here, or I'll go back in with you."

"No thanks. I'll take your word for it."

At that moment Delgado returned my call and I fumbled my way through the conventional greetings.

CONCLUSION

I spent the rest of that day and the entire one that followed thinking about nothing but how the case had ended. It was not only the tragic end of Rocco Cavaletti, but also that in the Agency we had called everything wrong about Carlos Fuentes. Maya seemed to be locked into the same circular mental process. We found little to say to each other beyond hello and goodbye. Unlike some others, this case had closed with no obvious symmetry or sense of resolution. It felt like a first attempt at writing a tragedy by an apprentice playwright, because no character had been purged of evil, no hero had been redeemed or elevated, no one had triumphed, and no one cheered at the end. Worse, but especially, no great truth or illuminating insight into the human condition had been revealed as the drama unraveled in a bleak and pointless ending.

It was more like an earthquake or a hurricane, a mindlessly destructive but frivolous gesture of nature, where if you inadvertently found yourself standing in the way of it, your life was snuffed out simply because you were there at the wrong moment. Still, neither did it feel spontaneous; the lethal conflict between Sebastian and Rocco could easily have been brewing beneath the surface for many years. And because that was the case, it at least had one characteristic of real tragedy; that when you saw it all, when it stood revealed in the final bloody scene, it felt *inevitable*. Witnessing it, you would utter that last word to yourself in a whisper, as I did that day when we were leaving Rocco's bedroom.

Having said that, Maya and I always resisted the idea that fate could be a force in our lives.

Some cases end with a feeling of both relief and release. This one only left us shaking our heads. I had called Mark Savio immediately after I told Delgado about finding Rocco's body, and Miss Rachel had been released after Delgado returned from securing the house five hours later. I knew from other cases that he would've offered her no apologies and she would probably not have accepted them if he had.

When I phoned later that day to congratulate her on her release she was somewhat less than cordial, even though I felt I had done what I set out to do, which was to get her out of jail with the charges dropped. Perhaps she thought, quite properly, that the Zacher Agency had played no direct role in restoring her freedom. After she made a special point of telling me that her Jack London cane had been restored to her, I turned her over to Maya to wrap up the billing issues.

I wondered briefly who would receive the ten percent of Cavaletti Vineyards that Rocco had owned, but that would only be one more detail in the approaching family shuffle. The next showdown would be between Miss Rachel and Luc. I couldn't predict the resolution of that encounter, but it might well resemble a previous struggle between Sebastian and Miss Rachel following the death of his father. A certain symmetry was evident there. We had heard nothing from Elizabeth, but that was her stance toward the world at large, with a few crude exceptions, as in our great room. Passive people are quickly overwhelmed in the tidal wave of events, and after witnessing her in her least passive mode, I didn't care to see her again at all.

The auto theft warrant against Carlos Fuentes had been withdrawn at the same time Miss Rachel was released, at the urging of the property manager. He was understandably eager to end this case with as little additional stress or publicity as possible. I heard from Rathbone that Carlos and Ximena were both back at work, as was the undamaged Mercedes E350 sedan. The butler was not able to speculate on whether they were a couple once again, but that reflected his manner of careful discretion. I knew otherwise, and Cody and I had not mentioned to anyone that Ximena was present when we attempted to capture Carlos in the abandoned clinic.

Even as I started to feel like I was moving on, I probably shouldn't have been surprised to receive a call from Celeste Howard three days after I thought everything was wrapped up. *Everything* is always a relative word, a loose net from which details fall easily through the spaces. I had already started on a huge landscape from a commission that came through my gallery, Galeria Uno, at a time when I was desperately ready to think about something other than the operatic, almost Oedipal sorrows of the Cavalettis. Not that they weren't real, but painting was always the ultimate escape for me into alternative realities. I always know how to locate that fantasy terrain when I need to, since it awaits me on the other side of one of the doors in my mind.

At first I wasn't eager to take a break for a social visit, but Celeste was very persuasive on the phone, as in life, and I couldn't help but wonder where she had now come to earth in this compound tragedy. After the straightforward suicide note from Rocco, I was now regarding Celeste as the loosest of loose ends.

The Cavaletti family was packing up at the mansion and would very soon be leaving for the States, she said. I wondered if she thought of that northern sanctuary as a safer place, as the media so often suggested. She told me that Delgado had returned their passports but offered no apology to any of them, saying only that he had done his duty in a crime committed by gringos against gringos. I could almost hear the flow of bottled water as, like Pontius Pilate, he washed his hands after a most elaborate shrug. As with anyone in this business, Diego Delgado had become an expert at moving on when the times called for it. I suspect that like the three of us in the Agency, he didn't spend a lot of time looking back.

The Cavaletti pilot was coming into León that night to take the family home in the morning, Celeste continued. Could I just have coffee with her to say a brief goodbye, after a situation that had created an extreme emotional drain on nearly everyone it touched? She would be happy to pay. In accepting her invitation, I couldn't help but wonder how much she had paid already. I could think of no one involved who had not, including all of us in the Agency. The long, angry red line traveling twelve inches down my thigh was healing nicely, but that was the least of my injuries.

On these terms, how could I not agree? This appeal made me think immediately of Ximena and Carlos, too. It really was about moving on. The truth was I didn't mind seeing Celeste without the cloud of suspicion of being a suspect over her head, although calling her ethical position cloudy would be far too kind at best. I saw it mainly as an opportunity to ask her a few tough questions of my own.

"Where would you like to meet?" I said,

knowing my voice held no great enthusiasm, since I wanted to give her no hope of escape. Maya was out working in the garden deadheading the azaleas, and I knew she wouldn't want to see Celeste again. The murder of Sebastian Cavaletti had not been her favorite case. In our latest conversation about it she had told me she was not ready to switch away from drinking our usual Chilean red, even though Luc had sent us a case of the 2004 Cavaletti Gran Reserva with a kind note written in a neat unshaking hand on the back of his business card. I couldn't help but contrast it with the previous Cavaletti note we had seen on the lid of Rocco's toilet seat.

Celeste suggested we connect at the coffee shop at the Fábrica La Aurora. She had arranged a ride, she said, and could meet me there at my convenience, but only if I could do it today.

The Fábrica is an old textile mill and shirt factory of great character that now houses a number of art galleries and antique shops, along with the coffee shop and a restaurant. It's a welcoming place for a quiet, wrap up kind of conversation. Perhaps Celeste realized that too.

I did not interrupt my painting, but at a certain point you have done the best part of your work for that day and you know it. I prefer not to ride it downward from there.

I walked inside the Fábrica, circling the fountain to travel the long central corridor that led to a small wandering courtyard with the outdoor coffee shop near the center. Seeing me as I approached, Celeste did not stand up, but only offered her hand palm downward when I reached the marble-topped table. When I took it briefly but without kissing it she said, "What an act of trust. You're so flexible."

"I thought this case was over." I smiled dimly, thinking of the scene in Rocco's bathroom.

"Just because Miss Rachel paid you? Some things are never over. They just grow into legend. Please have a seat with me."

A waitress in a white shirt and black pants with a sharp crease came to the table and we ordered two cappuccinos, mine with brown sugar and hers with a substitute. When she moved off toward the bar I pulled the silver chain with the amber pendant out of my shirt pocket and placed it in Celeste's palm.

"Thank you. I know where you must've found this. Having it back is almost symbolic of everything coming to an end now."

"That makes me want to examine the wrap-up process in more detail," I said. "Tell me how you look at it. This is your dance card today, where my name has suddenly appeared near the top, and not for the first time, as I recall. Your invitation surprised me this morning. I had already gone back to painting, and with no regrets, either. What will you do now? We all look down these roads from time to time, and certainly for you, there must be a fork coming into view."

"Well, yes, as it turns out. Mark Savio has made me an offer I can't refuse. I'm going to be the head receptionist in his San Francisco office. He's got two satellites as well, you know, in Walnut Creek and Sausalito." She looked like she'd just been named the new Junior Miss of the entire world.

"Déjà vu all over again. By golly." I tried to scrub all the traces of irony from my voice.

"Exactly."

"But you're going to be the head receptionist? Is there more than one? How many different ways can you greet someone who comes walking through the door?"

"Mark told me I would be the prettiest one."

I struggled to contradict this, but without seeing the others…such judgments are always subjective anyway. Maybe it was like being the receptionist at the entrance of a harem. Then something occurred to me.

"You and Mark Savio must've met before, am I right?"

"Of course, a couple of times or more when he came to see Miss Rachel at the vineyard."

Even then he would've popped up like a ten-point buck in Celeste's sights. "Will you be able to live in San Francisco on what that job pays?"

"As it happens, there are some interesting fringe

benefits. Mark has a big mansion in the Pacific Heights neighborhood. There's plenty of room for me, he says. It has eight bedrooms."

"I'm sure you'll use all of them. So the job comes with room and board. You do tend to land on your feet."

"Yes I do. That's my history, Paul, and that was Sebastian's style of generosity too. How about you?"

When the coffee arrived we paused for a moment, looking at each other over the white marble tabletop with a molded edge. It was set on a curvy steel base that reminded me of the furnishings in a French patisserie. Our chairs were done in the same design with a heart-shaped figure on the back.

"I land in a variety of ways, occasionally on my feet but sometimes on my ass and bleeding. But I do try to learn something each time. That's a good way to stay alive in this business, which is always my dream."

"I know you're a survivor," she went on. Celeste looked at me for a moment, as if she had thought of this before. "I don't come from anything, you know? Landing like this was always a dream for me too. I don't think my parents ever dream at all. They both drank the Kool-Aid and then asked for seconds."

This was harsh, but I didn't trip over it. "But how would you know that? Maybe they didn't tell you if they did. Dreams can be uncomfortable and might've made them nervous. Sometimes mine do if I dream about painting when it concerns a technique I haven't tried. What *did* they tell you about it?"

Celeste swept the napkin to the edge of the table and raised her left hand with the fingers widely spread. "What they told me read like a stop sign every single day. It was all about limits: Know your place, girl. You don't need to go to college because they don't teach you anything you can actually use and it costs too much. It's not real stuff and you'll end up in debt for your whole life. Find a good man and he'll take care of you. Don't ever try to be better than he is, even if he isn't the best guy you ever met. Make sure he's solid, though. The union will always protect your dad's job. If you marry a union guy you'll get that too.

"It was mostly quite old fashioned. Like, you can't fight city hall was another favorite of theirs. They believe in all of that. It was a good thing that I had the Internet and television so I could tell the outright lies from the plausible bullshit. At least I could look things up and get a different view."

"And we all know now there are no lies or bullshit on the Internet or television." I looked at her calmly.

"Whatever." She batted this away. "At least it got me out of there. That's my point. You probably didn't come from a small town in Wisconsin. You're probably hearing this for the first time."

"No. The small town of six thousand I came

from was in southeastern Ohio. Everyone thought they were cutting edge, especially my parents."

This was leading to nowhere enlightening. It was a beginning that did not imply the end. You can't deny a person's experience, and while leading a staid small town life in the Midwest had never been my ambition, we see so much vicious behavior in the cases the Zacher Agency gets involved with that I couldn't imagine Celeste had ever come close to the same kind of horror in her background. She didn't realize how much its absence was worth in terms of security and peace of mind. Although now, after her experience with the Cavalettis, maybe she was starting to get it. Maya could've told her in detail about many more examples of this—she had even walked out of my life for a while on our fourth case because of it.

Celeste stirred her coffee briefly and then finished it. "So what's your interest in doing these investigations? Miss Rachel said you're a pretty good painter, and I guess she knows something about art. She looked up your stuff online. She said you don't have to be a detective to make a living. You have a few choices, you know? More than I ever did in the past. My only choice was to escape rural Wisconsin or not."

"No, you're right. But the Agency does have some aspects that intrigue me mentally. I'm interested in the decisions people make. You know how sometimes people will say to you, 'Do the right thing!' All that means is you should do what they want you to do. But really doing the right thing is often much harder than it looks, because it can be difficult to know what the right thing is. I'm interested in the reasoning that goes into those choices."

Celeste gave me a skeptical smile. I was almost surprised I could still find some charm in it. "And do people often share their reasoning with you? Like, why would they want to? I don't think I ever would."

I could believe that, but I didn't expect a breakthrough now. "Sometimes they do. Often they don't have to because I can see their motives without them telling me anything. I've developed a fairly good eye over the years, and a decent ear for lies."

She studied my face for a while. "So you're most comfortable around shades of gray. You don't see the heroes and villains in life so much as the folks just trying to get by around the middle."

"And that's your neighborhood too?"

"Mostly."

"I also spend a lot of time there, because that's where most crime happens. As a challenge I once did a self-portrait in shades of gray that used no black pigment. The grays were all made from combinations of red and green mixed together with varying degrees of white."

"The reds cancel the greens, like a bad action

cancels a good," she said. It was comments like this that had made me warm to her in the past. Now, after the carnage, less so.

"Exactly. It's all in the subtleties like that. Some combinations were warm, some cool. You know all about that, don't you? I can see how good you are at mixing things up."

Her face grew more serious. "Now I think you're talking about Rocco. I knew this was coming, and I still asked you to meet me, didn't I? I'm not afraid of you, Paul."

"Yes, Rocco, among other things. What happened there? Maybe you and I can get into that, because for the law here in México, that's all been sorted out now. It's over and you're going home in the same condition you came in." This was a question I didn't think I'd get a chance to ask, but since she had invited me to this meeting…

"Yes, except for my job. Rocco got in over his head, that's all." A rueful shrug accompanied this. It was somewhat less than a signed confession of guilty involvement.

"But you encouraged him," I said. "I don't think going to bed with you was his idea."

Celeste was dressed quite modestly for that final meeting, in an outfit that showed little skin, as if to not encourage anyone else for a while. She was wearing a belted off-white dress with a straight skirt and a collar, with short sleeves.

"You probably don't know that I encourage a lot of men. Did you think you were the only one? It's a process I use to see who's interesting as well as who's interested. I encouraged you and it didn't take. Am I right?"

"Sure. That was an easy decision for me, since I was taken already. I was tempted, though, if that makes you feel any better. Anyway, now Rocco and his father are both dead. You knew Rocco killed Sebastian. It was because of his involvement with you." I knew that Delgado must've told her that too. He didn't have the habit of sparing anyone.

"I suppose I should've given Rocco a stress test before I went to bed with him." Her look hardened a bit more.

"Or even better, you could've been a more perceptive judge of character, or more committed to your patron."

Her expression did not change at all. "So, was I supposed to turn Rocco in when he told me what he had done? In bed he babbled like a baby. How loyal would that be? My natural inclination is to always be both loyal and discreet. For example, I never told Maya how much you wanted me. It was just short of drooling into my lap."

Without thinking I wiped my lips with a

napkin as I stared at her for a moment, searching without success for a snappy return. To get into the concept of selective loyalty with her at that moment would probably have ended the conversation, which in some ways I now wanted to do, but in others not. I was more interested in how she regarded herself and her role in this disaster. "Well, it's over now, whatever it was or might've been. You can cherish that. I don't know how you handle these things."

She made an offhand gesture. "I just go on, like I suspect most people do. And Rocco's remains were cremated too. It's tragic, I know. He and his dad will both be on the plane going back home tomorrow. I'm thinking of it as the ghost trip. We'll all be there, the same people that came down, maybe even in the same seats, but some will return in altered states." Her face was neutral. I read it more as veiled than simply resigned.

"But I guess you didn't cause that."

"No! I didn't." She arched forward like a snake about to strike across the table. "And I didn't make anybody do what they did, OK?" An indignant flush crossed her face but quickly faded. "No one can make anyone else do anything. I believe we all have to take responsibility for ourselves. Sebastian was always a hunter, and Rocco had been handed a victim's script that he'd been locked into since childhood. I was the only thing he ever went after that he thought was first class. When he told me that once in bed I was rather flattered. Wouldn't you be?"

She will never quit, I thought. She will never change because she can't allow herself to learn anything from what she does. "And then he discovered he couldn't handle being with you, that he was beneath it rather than equal to it," I said. "He had overreached himself, and he saw his father's shadow every time he looked into your eyes."

"I suppose that's true, although he was looking in many other places on my body, too. You have to feel you're worthy of something to enjoy it without guilt. Still, being with both him and his father never bothered me. They were such an interesting contrast of characters. But in the end they did it to themselves, didn't they? And the sad thing is they didn't have to. Don't you think we mostly tend to limit ourselves more than being held back by other people? That realization was what got me out of New Richmond, Wisconsin. I wasn't ever going to do that to myself."

"I can't deny that. So when did it begin with Rocco? Was it here?"

She shook her head. "About a week before we came down here. As we settled into the mansion, I could already feel it hanging in the air like extra baggage on the plane coming down, almost as if we couldn't hide it."

"Did you feel then it had been a mistake?"

"No. Mistakes are only things that end badly."

"And this didn't?"

"Not for me." Her bright smile was edged with an awkward look to her lips and her eyes avoided mine.

"I suppose the $50,000 bequest from Sebastian has helped you get some broader perspective on it. How did he find out about you and Rocco?"

"Sebastian was no fool and he guessed it not very long after we got here."

"Didn't it bother you that he thought you capable of that?"

"I don't think he ever wasted much time thinking about what I might be capable of, other than in bed. Not that Rocco could ever have been very cool about it. He was a wreck from the first time it happened. He couldn't look his dad in the eye."

"Did Sebastian think you belonged to him?"

"Absolutely, although he never mentioned Rocco to me. But that truly was the way he looked at all the women in his life. On that part I was not very smart, all right? I think you know something about women. I came on to Luc too but he just folded his arms and he wouldn't move an inch toward me. You know what people say—you can't control what happens, you can only control your reaction to it. He lived that line perfectly. Luc Cavaletti has never been out of control in his entire life."

I nodded slowly. "Sure, I can absolutely see that. Luc is the good soldier. He would never have taken up your offer, knowing you were also with his father, even if he didn't know about Rocco and he didn't mind cheating on his wife. Your move must've startled him more than anything. He always did his duty, and he will carry on nobly at the vineyard once Miss Rachel dies and he assumes control. Luc will emerge as the only worthy successor, even though he was not Sebastian's son."

Celeste's eyebrows went up. "So you know that too? You're even better than I thought."

"Not really. Rocco told me, as he must've told you."

"Yes, since being the only real Cavaletti son still did not make him the real successor to the vineyard, and he knew that every single day. He told me he woke up with it and he ate it for breakfast. His life experience was like his height; he was always coming up a little bit short of what was being asked of him."

"Not his fault," I said. "It was an existential failure. He was not born the man he needed to be, and because of that he lost to a worthier imposter."

"And Luc doesn't know he's an imposter."

"It doesn't matter," I said. "Like all the Cavalettis, like his father and Elizabeth and Miss Rachel, Luc has his own script too, and he's following it to the letter. I'm fully confident that he's going to be a natural for it, and he has the credential too. Now it's only you and I that know which part is a forgery."

"I won't tell if you don't."

"I never tell," I said, "except in our final report, which stays locked in our files."

Celeste gave me a conspiratorial smile and her hand touched mine very briefly.

As I look back now on that high summer day in early August, while I'm wrapping up my case notes in their final form, I find myself underlining some things, because Celeste seemed different then in notable ways. Although I couldn't have explained why or how, it made me smile as I worked. She was still frank when she spoke about her manner with men and her Wisconsin upbringing, but in a gentler way, looking back as she was. I suppose having escaped her background early on made it easier for her to be charitable about it. She also had a kind of softness in her manner that I hadn't observed before, except at the end when she clearly felt no responsibility for the way things played out. It made me wonder if she had always won men's interest by being tart and sassy. That might have been a good fit for her look and manner when she worked for Sebastian, given her equivocal position within the family, but it was not her style with me for that last meeting. I came away feeling satisfied that I was no longer one of her targets, but at the same time, wondering who might be next in line after

Mark Savio.

I have never been a hunter in the way Celeste so aptly described Sebastian, but I do enjoy meeting the women who play that role, and while they're not as numerous as the male hunters, they are more common than many more restrained women suspect. It may be that it's mostly men who have observed this, often at their own peril. In that sense, the case of the Cavaletti murder was certainly a cautionary tale, as most of them are.

This also makes me consider how well we can ever know each other. Maya and I often struggle after nearly ten years together. The upside is that we can still sometimes surprise each other and bring on a sly smile. And if Maya and I are hunters, we are mainly hunters for each other, searching out the undiscovered wonders that we never knew before.

It's almost easier to know ourselves, and that can be hard enough for most of us, even when we work at being honest. No wonder we rush past each other on the street so quickly, not looking into people's faces, avoiding their eyes, and veiling our expressions with a frowning mask of inner scrutiny merely as a routine defense against connecting with each other.

When we finished with our coffee that day, Celeste and I also brought to an end our brief and unconsummated connection too. We both sensed it was time to move on, and I was glad I'd accepted her invitation. I gave her a forceful look, one I can do well after so many cases. For me it was the wrap up. "Who are you, then, Celeste? What part of you is available, and what part of you is not? Availability can mask layers and layers beneath that are not so easy to access. I think of what I see in you as availability *lite*. It only goes so far."

She reached across the table and took my fingers in hers, softly this time. But prudently thinking of my huge landscape and the vigorous brushstrokes it demanded, I had only offered her my left hand. Attractive as she was, I would not allow Celeste Howard to leave any more marks on me. The damage was already healed and it had not left a scar. Her smile was at once welcoming and abstract. I thought it partly reflected a sense of frustration that she wished to explain or rationalize through a final, possibly prepared, statement. After all, this meeting was at her invitation, and I hadn't forgotten that.

"I'm glad you asked me that, Paul, because I think we probably won't ever meet again." She leaned across the table toward me, and her response was almost breathless. "I'm the one that got away. That's who I am and I want you to always remember me that way." She ended with an irresistible smile. Even now she was trying to leave a hook in me.

I smiled back at Celeste without irony. I had thought about this too, and I knew that she had gotten it exactly backwards. I was the one that got away, and I rose from the table with a subtle smile on my face, one that I knew neither Sebastian nor Rocco Cavaletti had ever been capable of.

Leaving the coffee shop of the Fábrica La Aurora I was thinking that people who don't realize how dangerous they are can be the most dangerous ones of all.

Walking back through the parking lot I spotted Carlos Fuentes bent over behind the wheel of the Mercedes working on his cell phone, so I took the long way around to avoid his eye. Of course, he was her driver for today's meeting. I didn't feel like interacting with anybody else, and he had never wanted to connect with me. In her final lines, Celeste had given me closure in a way nothing else in this case had. Like many people eager to talk about themselves, she had given me more information than she intended.

As I slid in behind the wheel and inserted the key I was still thinking about her, soon to be on her way back to California, to a lucrative job in a prestigious uptown law firm, to a berth in a Pacific Heights mansion in San Francisco, to an intimate connection with a man who thought he had suddenly gotten lucky in a place south of the border that he didn't care for much. Was it more than a bit beneath him? I couldn't help but imagine the life lesson Mark Savio had awaiting him, a lesson in no way connected with place. Celeste was always in motion, and she always landed on her feet. Although he would only prove to be the next stepping-stone to a higher goal, she was again, as she so much wished to be at each level, the clear winner. When in due course her footprints would be found on Mark Savio's back, it would not be from any Asian massage technique. How much time would pass before he realized they couldn't be washed away, even with tears?

As I drove away toward home on the Calzada de la Aurora, I wondered whether Rocco Cavaletti's ashes were even cold yet.

Feedback from readers is important, both in telling the author what he's doing right, and suggesting what might be done better. Please take a moment to post a brief review of this book on his Amazon pages.

Please visit the author's website at:
www.sanmiguelallendebooks.com